William Clark Russell

The Death Ship

a strange story - an account of a cruise in The Flying Dutchman - Vol. 1

William Clark Russell

The Death Ship
a strange story - an account of a cruise in The Flying Dutchman - Vol. 1

ISBN/EAN: 9783337302603

Printed in Europe, USA, Canada, Australia, Japan

Cover: Foto ©Andreas Hilbeck / pixelio.de

More available books at **www.hansebooks.com**

A STRANGE STORY;

AN ACCOUNT OF A CRUISE IN "THE FLYING DUTCHMAN," COLLECTED
FROM THE PAPERS OF THE LATE MR. GEOFFREY FENTON, OF POPLAR,
MASTER MARINER.

BY

W. CLARK RUSSELL,

AUTHOR OF
"THE WRECK OF THE GROSVENOR," "THE GOLDEN HOPE," "A SEA QUEEN,"
ETC., ETC.

IN THREE VOLUMES

VOL. I

LONDON
HURST AND BLACKETT, LIMITED
13, GREAT MARLBOROUGH STREET
1888

CONTENTS

OF

THE FIRST VOLUME.

———————•••———————

CONTENTS OF THE FIRST VOLUME.

THE DEATH SHIP.

CHAPTER I.

I WILL pass by all the explanations concerning the reasons of my going to sea, as I do not desire to forfeit your kind patience by letting this story stand. Enough if I say that after I had been fairly well grounded in English, arithmetic and the like, which plain education I have never wearied of improving by reading everything good that came in my way, I was bound apprentice to a respectable man named Joshua Cox, of Whitby, and

VOL. I.   B served my time in his vessel, the Laughing Susan—a brave, nimble brigantine.

We traded to Riga, Stockholm, and Baltic ports, and often to Rotterdam, where, having a quick ear, which has sometimes served me for playing upon the fiddle for my mates to dance or sing to, I picked up enough of Dutch to enable me to hold my own in conversing with a Hollander, or Hans Butterbox, as those people used to be called; that is to say, I had sufficient words at command to qualify me to follow what was said and to answer so as to be intelligible; the easier, since, uncouth as that language is, there is so much of it resembling ours in sound that many words in it might easily pass for portions of our tongue grossly and ludicrously articulated. Why I mention this will hereafter appear.

When my apprenticeship term had expired, I made two voyages as second mate, and then obtained an appointment to that post in a ship named the Saracen, for a voyage to the East Indies. This was *anno* 1796. I was then two-and-twenty years of age, a tall, well-built young fellow, with tawny hair, of the mariner's complexion from the high suns I had sailed under and the hardening gales I had stared into, with dark blue eyes filled with the light of an easy and naturally merry heart, white teeth, very regular, and a glad expression as though, forsooth, I found something gay and to like in all that I looked at. Indeed it, was a saying with my mother that "Geff,"— meaning Geoffrey—that "Geff's appearance was as though a very little joke would set the full measure of his spirits overflowing." But now, it is as an old poet finely wrote:

My golden locks time hath to silver turn'd,
(O time, too swift, and swiftness never ceasing!)
My youth, 'gainst age, and age at youth have spurn'd,
But spurn'd in vain!

And here it is but right to myself that I should say, though as a sailor I am but an obscure person, yet as a man I may claim some pride and lustre of descent, an ancestor being no less a worthy than one of the boldest of Queen Elizabeth's sea-captains and generals—Edward Fenton, I mean, who was himself of a sound and ancient Nottingham stock; illustrious for his behaviour against the Spaniards in 1588, and for his explorations of the hidden passage of the North Sea, mentioned with other notable matters in the Latin inscription upon his monument by Richard, Earl of Cork, who married his niece.

But enough of such parish talk.

The master of the Saracen was one Jacob Skevington, and the mate's name Christopher Hall. We sailed from Gravesend—for with Whitby I was now done—in the month of April, 1796. We were told to look to ourselves when we should arrive in the neighbourhood of the Cape of Good Hope, for it was rumoured that the Dutch, with the help

of the French, were likely to send a squadron
to recover Cape Town, that had fallen into
the hands of the British in the previous
September. However, at the time of our
lifting our anchor off Gravesend, the Cape
Settlement lay on the other side of the globe;
whatever danger there might be there, was
too remote to cast the least faint shadow upon
us; besides, the sailor was so used to the
perils of the enemy and the chase, that nothing
could put an element of uneasiness into his
plain, shipboard life, short of the assurance
of his own or his captain's eyes that the sail
that had hauled his wind and was fast growing upon the sea-line, was undeniably an
enemy's ship, heavily armed, and big enough
to cannonade him into staves.

So with resolved spirits, which many of us
had cheered and heartened by a few farewell
drams—for of all parts of the sea-faring life
the saying good-bye to those we love, and
whom the God of Heaven alone knows

whether we shall ever clasp to our breasts
again, is the hardest—we plied the capstan
with a will, raising the anchor to a chorus
that fetched an echo from the river's banks
up and down the Reach ; and then sheeting
home our topsails, dragging upon the halliards with piercing, far-sounding songs, we
gathered the weight of the pleasant sunny
wind into those spacious hollows, and in a
few minutes had started upon our long
journey.

Yet, though my parting with my friends
had not been of a nature to affect my spirits,
and though I was accounted to be, and indeed
was, a merry, careless fellow, I was sensible of
an unaccountable depression as, amidst the
duties which occupied me, I would cast
glances at the houses of Gravesend and the
shore sliding by, and hear, in momentary
hushes, tremulous tinkling sounds raised by
the water wrinkling, current-like under our
round and pushing bows.

CHAPTER II.

For days and days after we had cleared the Channel and entered upon those deep waters, which, off soundings sway in brilliant blue billows, sometimes paling into faint azure or weltering in dyes as purely dark as the violet, according as the mood of the sky is, nothing whatever of consequence befell. We were forty of a company. Captain Skevington was a stout but sedate sailor, who had used the sea for many years, and had confronted so many perils there was scarce an ocean-danger you could name about which he could not talk from personal experience. He was, likewise, a man of education and intelligence, with a manner about him at times not very intelligible, though his temper was always excellent and his skill as a seaman equal to every call made upon it. We carried six twelve-pounders and four brass swivels and a plentiful store of small-arms and ammunition. Our ship was five years old, a good sailer, handsomely found in all respects of sails and tackling, so that any prospect we might contemplate of falling in with privateers and such gentry troubled us little; since with a brave ship and nimble heels, high hot hearts, English cannon and jolly British beef for the working of them, the mariner need never doubt that the Lord will own him wherever he may go and whatever he may do.

We crossed the Equator in longitude thirty degrees west, then braced up to the Trade Wind that heeled us with a brisk gale in five degrees south latitude, and so skirted the sea in that great African bight 'twixt Cape

Palmas and the Cape of Good Hope, formerly called, and very properly, I think, the Ethiopic Ocean; for, though to be sure it is all Atlantic Ocean, yet, methinks, it is as fully entitled to a distinctive appellation as is the Bay of Biscay, that is equally one sea with that which rolls into it.

One morning in July, we being then somewhat south of the latitude of the island of St. Helena, a seaman who was on the topsail-yard hailed the deck, and cried out that there was a sail right ahead. It was an inexpressibly bright morning; the sun had been risen two hours, and he stood—a white flame of the blinding and burning brilliance he seems to catch up from the dazzling sands of Africa as he soars over them—in a sky of the most dainty sapphire fairness; not a cloud—no, not so big as a fading wreath of tobacco smoke anywhere visible, so that the ends of the sea went round with the clearness of the circle of a glass table, only that a small wind, very sweet and pleasant to every sense, blowing a little off our starboard bow, fluttered the ocean into a sort of hovering look, and its trembling caused the wake of the sun to resemble the leaping and frolicking of shoals of wet and sparkling mackerel.

We waited with much expectation and some anxiety for the stranger to approach near enough to enable us to gather her character, or even her nationality; for the experienced eye will always observe a something in the ships of the Dutch and French nations to distinguish the flags they belong to. It was soon evident that she was standing directly for us, shown by the speed with which her sails rose; but when her hull was fairly exposed, Captain Skevington, after a careful examination of her, declared her to be a vessel of about one hundred tons, probably a snow—her mainmast being in one with her foremast—and so we stood on, leaving it to her to be wary if she chose.

Whether she had at once made sure of us as an honest trader, I cannot say ; she never budged her helm by so much as the turn of a spoke, but came smoothly along, a very pretty shining object, rolling on the soft, long-drawn swell in such a way as to dart shadows across the moonlike gleaming of her canvas with the breathings of their full bosoms—so that the sight reminded me of the planet Venus as I once beheld her after she had passed from the tincture of the ruby into the quick light of the diamond, lightly troubled by the swift passage of a kind of gossamer scud, as though the winds on high sought to clothe her naked beauty with a delicate raiment of their own wearing, from which she was forever escaping into the liquid indigo she loves to float in.

After a little the English ensign was seen to flutter at her fore-topgallant-masthead. To this signal we instantly replied by hoisting our colour; and shortly after midday, arriving

abreast of each other, we backed our topsail-
yard, she doing the like, and so we lay
steady upon the calm sea, and so close, that
we could see the faces of her people over the
rail, and hear the sound, though not the
words, of the voice of the master giving his
orders.

It was Captain Skevington's intention to
board her, as he suspected she was from the
Indies, and capable therefore of giving us
some hints concerning the Dutch, into whose
waters, in a manner of speaking, we were
now entering; accordingly the jolly boat was
lowered and pulled away for the stranger,
that proved to be the snow, Lovely Nancy,
of Plymouth—name of cruel omen as I shall
always deem it, though I must ever love the
name of Nancy as being that of a fair-haired
sister who died in her fifteenth year.

As many of my readers may not be acquainted with sea terms, it may be fit to say
here, that a snow is nothing more than a

brig, with the trifling addition of a thin mast
abaft her mainmast, upon which her trysail
or boom mainsail sets. I guess these vessels
will always bear this name until their trysail-
masts go out of fashion.

But to return.

I know not why I should have stood looking very longingly at that Plymouth ship
whilst our captain was on board her; for
though to be sure we had now been at sea
since April, whilst she was homeward bound,
yet I was well satisfied with the Saracen and
all on board. I was glad to be getting a
living and earning in wages money enough
to put away; my dream being to save so
much as would procure me an interest in a
ship, for out of such slender beginnings have
sprung many renowned merchant princes in
this country. But so it was. My heart
yearned for that snow as though I had a
sweetheart on board. Even Mr. Hall, the
mate, a plain, literal, practical seaman, with

as much sentiment in him as you may find in
the first Dutchman you meet in the Amsterdam fish-market, even he noticed my wistful
eyes, and clapping me on the back, cries
out—

"Why, Fenton, my lad, I believe you'd be
glad to go home in that little wagon yonder
if the captain would let ye."

" I believe I would, sir," I replied ; "and
yet if I could, I don't know that I would,
either."

He laughed and turned away, ridiculing
what he reckoned a piece of lady-like sentiment ; and that it was no more, I daresay I
was as sure as he, though I wished the
depression at the devil, for it caused me to
feel, whilst it was on me, as though a considerable slice of my manhood had slipped
away overboard.

It is one of the few pleasures time permits
to old men to recall the sweet, or gay, or fair
pictures which charmed them when young.

And which of all our faculties is more wonderful as a piece of mechanism, and more Divine in its life-giving properties, than Memory, which enables the Spirit to quicken dust that has lain for many years in the womb of time; to attire it and to return to it its passions, emotions, and all other qualities; to put back the cycles the sun has run and oblige him to shine on forms which were then infants, but are now grass-hidden ridges ; on houses then stately but now long since swept away ; on meadows and orchards then bright with daisies, ruddy with fruit, but now covered with houses and busy streets whose side-walks echo to the tread of generations more dream-like in that past to which the aged eye turns than ever can be the dead who then lived.

'Tis thus when I think of that Plymouth snow ; for leaning back in my chair and closing these eyes, that morning shines all around me; the tremulous sea of blue, of a satin sheen in its tiny ripplings, shot with milder tints where the currents run as though they were the thin fingers of the wind toying with the bosom of the deep, bends to the distant sky upon whose lowermost reaches it flings the same opal lustre it gathers at its horizon ; the air blows fitfully, like the warm breathings from a woman's sweet lips, and sometimes stills our sails and sometimes suffers them to flutter in sounds soothing as the murmurs of a midsummer night breeze amid the high branches of a sleeping oak. The snow had black sides but was painted white from her water-line ; and though there was no lack of draining weeds and clustered shells upon her bilge and run, yet, with every slow roll from us, the wet whiteness, taking the meridian effulgence, broke out in a glory as of virgin silver, enriched by the marine adhesions, into the very likeness of a re-splendent mosaic of precious metal and green glass.

Such magic has the sea to beautify whatever it is permitted to possess long enough
for its powers of enrichment to work their
way!

Her canvas flashed out of shadow into
brightness with every lift of the swell; the
ripples ran a dissolving tracery along her
bends, as dainty to see as the choicest lace;
the weather-clouded faces of her men looked
at us over the stout bulwark-rail that was
broken by a few open ports through which
you spied the mouths of little cannon ; and it
was laughable to mark her figurehead, that
represented an admiral in a cocked hat—a
cheap dockyard purchase, no doubt, for the
effigy was ridiculously out of character and
foolishly too big for the vessel—bowing to
the blue surface that flowed in lines of
azure light to the cutwater, as though there
were some mermaid there to whom he would
be glad to " make a leg," as the old saying
was.

CHAPTER III.

THE CAPTAIN AND I TALK OF THE DEATH SHIP.

AFTER three-quarters-of-an-hour, or there-abouts, Captain Skevington returned. We then trimmed to our course again, and, ere long, the Plymouth snow was astern of us, rolling her spread of canvas in a saluting way that was like a flourish of farewell.

Whilst the jolly boat was being hoisted, the captain stood gazing at the snow with a very thoughtful face, and then burying his hands in his pockets, he took several turns up and down the deck with his head bowed, and his whole manner not a little grave. He presently went to the mate, and talked with him, but it looked as though Mr. Hall found little to raise concern in what the captain said, as he often smiled, and once or twice broke into a laugh that seemed to provoke a kind of remonstrance from the master, who yet acted as though he were but half in earnest too ; but they stood too far away for me to catch a syllable of their talk.

It was my watch below at eight o'clock that evening.   I was sitting alone in the cabin, sipping a glass of rum and water, ready to go to bed when I had swallowed the dose.   There was but one lamp, hanging from a midship beam, and the cabin was somewhat darksome.   The general gloom was deepened by the bulkhead being of a sombre, walnut colour, without any relief— such as probably would have been furnished had we carried passengers—from table-glass or silver, or such furniture.   I mention these matters because they gave their complexion to the talk I am now to repeat.

Presently, down into this interior through

the companion hatch comes Captain Skevington. I drained my glass and rose to
withdraw.

"Stop a minute, Fenton," says he; "what
have you been drinking there?"

I told him.

"Another drop can't hurt you," said he;
"you have four hours to sleep it off in."
With which he called to the boy to bring him
a bottle of brandy from his cabin. He bid
me help myself whilst he lighted a pipe of
tobacco, and then said: "The master of the
snow we met to-day warns us to keep a
bright look-out for the Dutch. He told me
that yesterday he spoke an American ship
that was short of flour, and learnt from the
Yankee—though how Jonathan got the news
I don't know—that there's a Dutch squadron
making for the Cape, in charge of Admiral
Lucas, and that among the ships is the Dor-
drecht of sixty-six guns and two forty-gun
frigates."

" But should we fall in with them will they meddle with us, do you think, sir ?" said I.

" Beyond question," he answered.

" Then," said I, " there is nothing for it but to keep a sharp look-out. We have heels, anyway."

He smoked his pipe with a serious face, as though not heeding me ; then looking at me steadfastly, he exclaimed, " Fenton, you've been a bit of a reader in your time, I believe. Did your appetite that way ever bring you to dip into magic, necromancy, the Black Art, and the like of such stuff ?"

He asked me this with a certain strangeness of expression in his eyes, and I thought it proper to fall into his humour. So I replied that in the course of my reading I might have come across hints of such things, but that I had given them too little attention to qualify me to reason about them or to form an opinion.

" I recollect when I was a lad," said he,

passing my answer by, so to speak, "hearing
an old lady that was related to my mother,
tell of a trick that was formerly practised and
credited, too ; a person stood at a grave and
invoked the dead, who made answer."

I smiled, thinking that only an old woman
would talk thus.

"Stop!" cried he, but without temper.
"She said it was common for a necromancer
to invoke and obtain replies; but that though
answers were returned, they were not spoken
by the dead, but by the Devil. The proof
being that death is a separation of the soul
from the body, that the immortal soul cannot
inhabit the corpse that is mere dust, that
therefore the dead cannot speak, themselves,
but that the voices which seem to proceed
from them are uttered by the Evil One."

"Why the Evil One?" said I.

" Because he delights in whatever is out of
nature, and in doing violence to the har-
monious fabric of the universe."

" That sounds like a good argument, sir,"
said I, still smiling.

" But," continued he, " suppose the case
of men now living, though by the laws of
Nature they should have died long since.
Would you say that they exist as a corpse
does when invoked—that is, by the possession and voice of the Devil, or that they
are informed by the same souls which were
in them when they uttered their first cry in
this life."

" Why, sir," I answered, " seeing that the
soul is immortal, there is no reason why it
should not go on inhabiting the clay it
belongs to, so long as that clay continues
to possess the physical power to be moved
and controlled by it."

" That's a shrewd view," said he, seemingly
well-pleased. " But see here, my lad ! our
bodies are built to last three score and ten
years. Some linger to an hundred ; but so
few beyond, that every month of continued

being renders them more and more a sort of prodigies. As the end of a long life approaches—say a life of ninety years—there is such decay, such dry-rot, that the whole frame is but one remove from ashes. Now, suppose there should be men living who are known to be at least a hundred and fifty years old—nay, add an average of forty to each man and call them one hundred and ninety years old—but who yet exhibit no signs of mortality; would not you say that the bounds of Nature having been long since passed, their bodies are virtually corpses, imitating life by a semblance of soul that is properly the voice and possession of the Devil?"

" How about Methusaleh, and others of those ancient times?"

" I'm talking of to-day," he answered. "'Tis like turning up the soil to work back into ancient history; you come across things which there's no making anything of."

"But what man is there now living who has reached to a hundred-and-ninety?" cried I, still struck by his look, yet, in spite of that, wondering at his gravity, for there was a determination in his manner of reasoning that made me see he was in earnest.

"Well," said he, smoking very slowly, "the master of that snow, one Samuel Bullock, of Rotherhithe, whom I recollect as mate of a privateer some time since, told me that when he was off the Agulhas Bank, he made out a sail upon his starboard bow, braced up, and standing west-sou'-west. There was something so unusual and surprising about her rig that the probability of her being an enemy went clean out of his mind, and he held on, influenced by the sort of curiosity a man might feel who follows a sheeted figure at night, not liking the job, yet constrained to it by sheer force of unnatural relish. 'Twas the first dogwatch; the sun drawing down; but daylight was

yet abroad, when the stranger was within
hail upon their starboard quarter, keeping
a close luff, yet points off, on account of the
antique fit of her canvas.   Bullock, as he
talked, fell a-trembling, though no stouter-
hearted man sails the ocean, and I could see
the memory of the thing working in him like
a bloody conscience.   He cried out, 'May
the bountiful God grant that my ship reaches
home in safety!'   I said, 'What vessel was
she, think you?'   'Why, captain,' says he,
'what but the vessel which 'tis God's will
should continue sailing about these seas?'   I
started to hear this, and asked if he saw
any of the crew.   He replied that only two
men were to be seen—one steering at a
long tiller on the poop deck, and the other
pacing near him on the weather side.   'I
seized the glass,' said he, 'and knelt down,
that those I viewed should not observe me,
and plainly catched the face of him who
walked.'"

"How did Bullock describe him, sir?" said I.

"He said he wore a great beard and was very tall, and that he was like a man that had died and that when dug up preserved his death-bed aspect; he was like such a corpse artificially animated, and most terrible to behold from his suggestions of death-in-life. I pressed him to tell me more, but he is a person scanty of words for the want of learning. However, his fears were the clearest relation he could give me of what he had seen."

"It was the Phantom Ship he saw, you think, sir?" said I.

"I am sure. He bid me dread the sight of it more than the combined navies of the French and the Dutch. The apparition was encountered in latitude twenty miles south of thirty-six degrees. 'Tis a spectre to be shunned, Fenton, though it cost us every rag of sail we own to keep clear."

"Then what you would say, captain,"
said I, "is, that the people who work that
ship have ceased to be living men by reason
of their great age, which exceeds by many
years our bodies' capacity of wear and tear;
and that they are actually corpses influenced
by the Devil—who is warranted by the same
Divine permission we find recorded in the
Book of Job, to pursue frightful and unholy
ends?"

'It is the only rational view," he answered.
"If the Phantom Ship be still afloat, and
navigated by a crew, they cannot be men
in the sense that this ship's company are
men."

"Well, sir," said I, cheerfully, "I reckon
it will be all one whether they be fiends,
or flesh and blood miraculously wrought to
last unto the world's end, for it is a million
to nothing that we don't meet her. The
Southern Ocean is a mighty sea, a ship is
but a little speck, and once we get the Mada-

gascar coast on our bow we shall be out of the Death Ship's preserves."

However, to my surprise, I found that he maintained a very earnest posture of mind in this matter. To begin with, he did not in the least question the existence of the Dutch craft; he had never beheld her, but he knew those who had, and related tales of dismal issues of such encounters. The notion that the crew were corpses, animated into a mocking similitude of life, was strongly infixed in his mind; and he obliged me to tell him all that I could remember of magical, ghostly, supernatural circumstances I had read about or heard of, until I noticed it was half-an-hour after nine, and that, at this rate, my watch on deck would come round before I had had a wink of sleep.

However, though I went to my cabin, it was not to rest. I lay for nearly two hours wide awake. No doubt the depression I had marked in myself had exactly fitted my mind for such fancies as the captain had talked about. It was indeed impossible that I should soberly accept his extraordinary view touching the endevilment of the crew of the Death Ship. Moreover, I hope I am too good a Christian to believe in that Satyr which was the coinage of crazy, fanatical heads in the Dark Ages, that cheaply-imagined Foul Fiend created to terrify the weak-minded with a vision of split-hoofs, legs like a beast's, a barbed tail, flaming eyes, and nostrils discharging the sickening fumes of sulphur.

But concerning the Phantom Ship herself— the Flying Dutchman as she has been styled —'tis a spectre that has too often crossed the path of the mariner to admit of its existence being questioned. If there be spirits on land, why not at sea, too ? There are scores who believe in apparitions, not on the evidence of their own eyes—they may never have beheld such a sight—but on the testimony of wit-

nesses sound in their religion and of unassail-
able integrity ; and why should we not accept
the assurance of plain, honest sailors, that
there may be occasionally encountered off the
Agulhas Bank, and upon the southern and
eastern coast of the African extremity, a wild
and ancient fabric, rigged after a fashion long
fallen into disuse, and manned by a crew
figured as presenting something of the aspect
of death in their unholy and monstrous
vitality ?

I turned this matter freely over in my
mind as I lay in my little cabin, my thoughts
finding a melancholy musical setting in the
melodious sobbing of water washing past
under the open port, and snatching distressful
impulses from the gloom about me, that was
rendered cloud-like by the moon who was
climbing above our mastheads, and clothing
the vast placid scene outside with the beauty
of her icy light ; and then at seven bells
fell asleep, but was called half - an - hour

later, at midnight, to relieve Mr. Hall,
whose four hours' spell below had come
round.

CHAPTER IV.

WE talked occasionally of the Phantom Ship after this for a few days, the captain on one occasion, to my surprise, producing an old volume on magic and sorcery which it seems he had, along with an odd collection of books, in his cabin, and arguing and reasoning out of it. But he never spoke of this thing in the presence of the mate who, to be sure, was a simple, downright man, without the least imaginable flavour of imagination to render sapid the lean austerity of his thoughts, and who, therefore, as you may suppose, as little credited the stories told of the Dutchman's ship as the Ebrew Jew believes in our Lord

Hence, as there were but the captain and

me to keep this shuttlecock of a fancy flying,
it fluttered before long to the ground ;
perhaps the quicker, because on the Sunday
following our speaking with the Plymouth
snow, there happened a piece of work, sharp
and real enough to drive all ideas of visions
and phantasms out of our heads.

It was ten o'clock in the morning when a
sail was descried broad on the larboard beam.
We gave her no heed at first. It being the
Sabbath, and a warm sweet morning, the
men having nothing to do, hung about the
decks, smoking, telling stories and the like ;
and being cleanly attired in jackets and white
trousers, they contributed a choice detail to
the general structure of well - kept decks,
shining brass work, massive shrouds soaring
from the black dead-eyes to the great round
tops, with further rigging of a similar kind
ruling the topmasts to the cross-trees, and
on yet to the topgallant heights, ropes cross-
ing ropes and ratline following ratline, till the

tracery, both in its substance aloft and its shadows below and in the inclined hollows of the sails, puzzled the eye with the complexity of a spider's web ; whilst from the water-ways to the lower yard-arms and thence to the ends of the yards above, mounted the vast sheets of canvas, each central surface arching in snow to the raining light of the sun, like the fair full breasts of a virgin, passed the taut bolt-ropes, narrowing as they rose till, the royal-yards being reached, the sails there swelled yearning skywards as though they were portions of the prismatic ribbed and pearly beds of cloud directly over the ship, rent from them by the sweep of our trucks and knitted by our seamen to those lofty spars.

It was not long, however, before we made out that the vessel down in the eastern quarter was steering large, and at the time the appearance of her canvas assured us of this, she slackened away her larboard braces to head up for us, hauling upon a bowline with a suddenness that left her intention to parley with us questionless.

We hoisted the English ensign and held on a bit, viewing her with an intentness that brought many of our eyes to a squint ; then the captain, observing that she showed no colours and was a big ship, put his helm up for a run.

No sooner had we braced in our yards, when the fellow behind us squared away too, and threw out lower and topmast studding-sails with a rapidity that satisfied us she was a man-of-war, apparently a liner. This notion, joined to the belief that she was a Dutchman, was start enough for us all. Our small company were not likely to hold their own against the disciplined masses of a two or three decker, even though she should prove a Spaniard. Our guns were too few to do anything with tiers of batteries heavy enough to blow us out of water. So as there was nothing for it but a fair trial of speed, we sprung to our work like hounds newly unleashed, got her dead before it, ran out studding-sail booms on both sides and sent the sails aloft soaking wet for the serviceableness of the weight the wetness would give, and stationing men in the tops and cross-trees we whipped up buckets of water to them, with which they drenched the canvas, till our cloths must have looked as dark as a collier's to the ship astern of us.

It was very slow work at first, and we were thankful for that; for every hour carried us nearer to the night into which the moon now entered so late and glowed with such little power, even when she had floated high, that we could count, after sundown, upon several hours of darkness; but it was not long before it became evident to us all that, spite of the ceaseless wetting of our sails, the ship in our wake was growing. Then, satisfied of her superiority, and convinced of our nationality,

she let fly a forecastle gun at us, of the ball
of which we saw nothing, and hoisted the
Dutch colours at her fore-royal masthead,
where, at all events, we could not fail to
distinguish the flag.

"Confound such luck!" cries Skevington
at this. "How can our apple-bows contend
with those pyramids of sails there? What's
to be done?" he says, as if thinking aloud.
"It's clear she's our master in running, and
I fear she'll be more than our match on
a bowline — with the weather gage too!
And yet, by the thunder of Heaven, Mr.
Hall, it does go against the current of any
sort of English blood to haul down that
piece of bunting there," says he, casting his
eyes at the peak where our flag was blowing,
'to the command of a Dutchman's cannon!"

"The wind's coming away more easterly,"
said the mate, with a slow turning of his gaze
into the quarter he mentioned, "and it'll be
breezing up presently, if there's any significa-

tion in the darker blue of the sea that way."

It happened as he said ; but the Dutchman got the first slant of it, and you saw the harder pulling of his canvas in the rounded rigidity of light upon the cloths, whilst the dusky line of the wind, followed by the flashings of the small seas, whose leaping heads it showered into spray, was yet approaching our languid ship, whose lower and heavy canvas often flapped in the weak air.

A couple of shot came flying after us from the man-of-war's bowchasers ere the breeze swept to our spars ; and now the silvery line of the white water that her stem was hewing up and sending in a brilliant whirl past her was easy do be seen; aye, 'twas even possible to make out the very lines of her reef-points upon the fore-course and topsail, whilst through the glass you could discern groups of men stationed upon her forecastle, and mark some quarter-deck figure now and again

impatiently bound on to the rail and over-
hang it like a davit, with an arm round a
backstay, in his eagerness to see how fast
they were coming up with us.

With all element of terror in it extinguished
by time, it is a sight to recall with a sailor's
fondness; for indeed the Dutchman was a
fine ship, very tall, with port-lids painted red
inside, so that with the guns projecting from
them, in two tiers, the aspect was that of
rows of crimson, wolfish jaws, every beast
with his tongue out; her yards were immensely square, and her studding-sail booms
extending great spaces of canvas far over the
side, she showed upon the dark blue frothing
ocean like some Heaven-seeking hill, fleecily
clad with snow to twenty feet above the
water-line, where it was black rock down to
the wash of the froth. In the freshening
wind, as it came up to us, I seemed to catch
an echo of the drum-like roll of the brisken-
ing gale in those airy heights, and to hear the

seething of the boiling stuff at her forefoot.
But, thanks be to Heaven, there was now a
swift racing of foam from under our counter,
whence it streamed away with a noise deli-
cious to hearken to, as though it was the
singing of the rain of a thunder-cloud upon
hard land ; for whenever the breeze gathered
its weight in our canvas the Saracen sprang
from it meteor-fashion, and away we sped
with helm right amidships, and the wind
flashing fair over the taffrail.

The excitement of this chase was deep in
us when the captain gave orders to train a
couple of guns aft and to continue firing at
the pursuing craft; which was done, the
powder-smoke blowing like prodigious glis-
tening cobwebs into our canvas forward.
Meanwhile, the English colours flew hardily
at our peak, whilst preventer guys were
clapped on the swinging-booms and other
gear added to give strength aloft; for the
wind was increasing as if by magic, the

ribbed clouds had broken up and large bodies of vapour were sailing overhead with many ivory-white shoulders crowding upon the horizon, and the strain upon the studding-sail tacks was extremely heavy. But you saw that it was Captain Skevington's intention to make the Saracen drag what she could not carry, and to let what chose blow away before he started a rope-yarn, whilst we had that monster astern there sticking to our skirts; and by this time it was manifest that with real weight in the wind our heels were pretty nearly as keen as hers, which made us hope that should the breeze freshen yet we might eventually get away.

Well, at three o'clock it was blowing downright hard, though the weather was fine, the heavens mottled, the clouds being compacted and sailing higher, stormy in complexion and moving slowly; the sea had grown hollow and was most gloriously violet in colour, with plumes of snow, which curled to the gale on the head of each liquid courser; the sun was over our fore-topgallant yard-arm and showered down his glory so as to form a golden weltering road for us to steer beside.   The ship behind catched his light and looked to be chasing us on wings of yellow silk.   But never since her keel had been laid had the Saracen been so driven.   The waters boiled up to the black-faced turbaned figure under the bowsprit, and from aft I could sometimes observe the glassy curve of the bow sea, arching away for fathoms forward, showing plain through the headrails.   A couple of hands hung grinding upon the wheel with set teeth, and the sinews in their naked arms stood out like cords; others were at the relieving-tackles; and through it we pelted, raising about us a bubbled, spuming and hissing surface that might have answered to the passage of a whirlwind, repeatedly firing at the Dutch man-of-war when the heave of the surge gave us the chance, and noticing the constant flash in his bows and the white smother that blew along with him, though the balls of neither appeared to touch the other of us.

Yet, that we should have been ultimately overhauled and brought to a stand I fully believe but for a providential disaster. For no matter how dark the dusk may have drawn around at sundown, the Dutchman was too close to us to miss the loom of the great press of canvas we should be forced to carry: at least, so I hold; and then, again, there was the consideration of the wind failing us with the coming of the stars, for we were still in the gentle parallels. But let all have been as it might, I had just noted the lightning-like wink of one of the enemy's fore-chasers, when to my exceeding amazement, ere the ball of smoke could be shredded into lengths by the gale, I observed the whole fabric of the Dutchman's towering foremast, with the great course, swelling

topsail, topgallant-sail and royal, and the
fore-topmast staysail and jibs melt away as
an icicle approached by flame ; and in a
breath, it seemed, the huge ship swung
round, pitching and foaming after the manner
of a harpooned whale, with her broadside
to us, exhibiting the whole fore-part of her
most greviously and astonishingly wrecked.

A mighty cheer went up from our decks at
the sight, and there was a deal of clapping of
hands and laughter. Captain Skevington
seized the telescope, and talked as he worked
away with it.

" A rotten foremast, by the thunder of
Heaven !" he cried, using his favourite adju-
ration ; " it could be nothing else. No shot
our guns throw could work such havoc. By
the height that's left standing the spar has
fetched away close under the top. And the
mess ! the mess !"

With the naked eye one could see that.
The foremast had broken in twain ; its fall

had snapped off the jibbooms to the bowsprit
cap, and I do not doubt a nearer view would
have shown us the bowsprit itself severely
wrenched. I could not imagine the like of
that picture of confusion—her studding-sails,
having been set on both sides, drowned all
her forward part in canvas, a goodly portion
of which had been torn into rags by the fall;
immense stretches of sail lay in the water,
sinking and rising with the rolling of the
ship, and dragging her head to the wind; her
main topmast studding-sails, and all the
canvas on that mast and the mizzen—the
yards lying square—were shaking furiously,
owing to the posture in which she had fallen;
every moment this terrible slatting threatened
her other spars; and it needed not a sailor's
imagination to conceive how fearfully all that
thunderous commotion aloft must heighten
the distracting tumult on deck, the passionate
volleys of commands, the hollow shocks of
seas smiting the inert hull, the shouting of

the seamen, and, as we might be sure, the cries and groans of the many upon whom that soaring fabric of yards, sails, and rigging had fallen with the suddenness of an electric bolt from the clouds.

For a whole hour after this we touched not a rope, leaving our ship to rush from the Dutchman straight as an arrow from a bow. But, Lord!—the storming aloft!—the fierce straining of our canvas till tacks and guys, sheets and braces rang out upon the wind like the clanking of bells, to a strain upon them tauter than that of harp-strings; the boiling noises of the seas all about our bow and under our counter, where the great bodies of foam roared away into our wake, as the white torrent raves along its bed from the foot of a high cataract! There was an excitement in this speed and triumph of escape from what must have proved a heavy and inglorious disaster to us all which put fire into the blood, and never could I have imagined how

sentient a ship is, how participent of what
stirs the minds of those she carries, until I
marked the magnificent eagerness of our
vessel's flight—her headlong domination of
the large billows which underran her, and the
marble-hard distention of her sails, reminding
you of the tense cheeks of one who holds his
breath in a run for his life.

Distance and the sinking of the sun, and
the shadows which throng sharply upon his
heels in these climes, left the horizon in
course bare to our most searching gaze. We
then shortened sail, and under easy canvas,
we put our helm a-lee, and stood north-
wards on a bowline until midnight, when we
rounded in upon our weather-braces and
steered easterly, Captain Skevington suspect-
ing that the Dutchman would make all haste
to refit and head south under some jury con-
trivance, in the expectation that as we were
bound that way when he fell in with us so
we should haul to our course afresh when we

lost sight of him. Yet in the end we saw him no more, and what ship he was I never contrived to learn ; but certainly it was an extraordinary escape, though whether due to our shot, or to his foremast being rotten, or to its having been sprung and badly fished, or to some earlier wound during an engagement, must be left to conjecture.

CHAPTER V.

BUT though, after this piece of severe reality,
Captain Skevington had very little to say
about such elusive and visionary matters as
had before engaged us, it was clear from
some words which he let fall that he re-
garded our meeting with the Dutch battle-
ship as a sort of reflected ill-luck from the
snow that had passed the Phantom Dutchman, and the idea possessing him — as
indeed it had seized upon me — that the
Lovely Nancy was sure to meet with mis-
adventure, and might have the power of
injuring the fortune of any vessel that spoke
with her intimately, as we had, caused him

to navigate the ship with extraordinary
wariness. A man was constantly kept aloft
to watch the horizon, and repeatedly hailed
from the deck that we might know he
was awake to his work; other sharp-eyed
seamen were stationed on the forecastle; at
night every light was screened, so that we
moved along like a blot of liquid pitch upon
the darkness. On several occasions I heard
Captain Skevington say that he would sooner
have parted with twenty guineas than have
boarded, or had anything to do with, the
snow. Happily, the adventure with the
Dutchman led the seamen to suppose that
the master's anxiety wholly concerned the
ships of the enemy; for had it got forward
that the Lovely Nancy had sighted Vanderdecken's craft off the Agulhas, I don't
question that they would have concluded our
meeting with the snow boded no good to us,
that we were likely ourselves to encounter the
spectral ship—if indeed she were a phantasm,

and not a substantial fabric, as I myself deemed—and so perhaps have refused to work the Saracen beyond Table Bay.

At that Settlement it was necessary we should call for water, fresh provisions and the like ; and on the sixth of July, in the year 1796, we safely entered the Bay and let go our anchor, nothing of the least consequence to us having happened since we were chased, the weather being fine with light winds ever since the strong breeze before which we had had run, died away.

After eighty-one days of sea and sky the meanest land would have offered a noble refreshment to our gaze ; judge then of the delight we found in beholding the royal and ample scenery of as fair and spacious a haven as this globe has to offer. But as Captain George Shelvocke, in the capital account he wrote of his voyage round the world in 1718, there points out, the Cape of Good Hope, by which he must intend Table Bay, has been so often described, that, says he, "I can say nothing of it that has not been said by most who have been here before."

We lay very quietly for a fortnight, feeling perfectly secure, as you may conclude when I tell you that just round the corner, that is to say, in Simon's Bay, there were anchored no less than fourteen British ships of war, in command of Vice-Admiral Sir George Elphinstone, of which two were seventy-fours, whilst five mounted sixty-four guns each. Meeting one of the captains of this squadron, Captain Skevington told him how we had been chased by a Dutch liner, and the replied he did not doubt it was one of he vessels who were coming to retake—if they could—the settlement we had captured from the nation that had established the place. But I do not think the notion probable, as the Dutch ships did not show themselves off Saldanha Bay for some weeks after we had sailed.

This, however, is a matter of no moment whatever.

We filled our water casks, laid in a plentiful stock of tobacco, vegetables, hogs, poultry, and such produce as the country yielded, and on the morning of the eighteenth of July hove short, with a crew diminished by the loss of one man only, a boatswain's mate, named Turner, who, because we suffered none of the men to go ashore for dread of their deserting the ship, slipped down the cable on the night of our departure, and swam to the beach naked with some silver pieces tied round him in a handkerchief. Behold the character of the sailor ! For a few hours of such drunken jollity as he may obtain in the tavern and amid low company, he will be content to forfeit all he has in the world. It was known that this man Turner had a wife and two children at home dependent upon his earnings ; yet no thoughts of them could suppress his deplorable, restless spirit. But I afterwards heard he was punished even beyond his deserts ; for being pretty near spent by his swim, he lay down to sleep, but was presently awakened by something crawling over him that proved a venomous snake called a puff-adder, which, on his moving, stung him, whereof he died.

It was the stormy season of the year off South Africa ; but, then, a few days of westerly winds would blow us into mild and quiet zones, and, come what might, the ship we stood on was stout and honest, all things right and true aloft, the provision-space hospitably stocked, and the health of the crew of the best.

'Twas a perfectly quiet, cheerful morning when we manned the capstan ; the waters of the bay stretched in an exquisite blue calm to the sandy wastes on the Blaawberg side, and thence to where the town stands ; the atmosphere had the purity of the object-lens of a perspective glass, and the far distant

Hottentot Holland Mountains, with summits so mighty that the sky appeared to rest upon them, gathered to their giant slopes such a mellowness and richness of blue, that they showed as a dark atmospheric dye which had run and stained before being stanched, that part of the heavens, rather than as prodigious masses of land of the usual complexion of mountains when viewed closely. That imperial height called Table Mountain, guarded by the amber-tinted couchant lion, reared a marvellously clear sky-line, and there the firmament appeared as a flowing sea of blue, flushing its full cerulean bosom to the flat altitude as though it would overflow it. But I noticed a shred of crawling vapour gather up there whilst the crew were chorussing at the capstan, and by the time our topsails were sheeted home there was a mass of white vapour some hundred feet in depth, foaming and churning atop, with delicate wings of it circling out into the blue, where they gyrated like butterflies and melted. The air was full of the moaning noises of the south-east wind flying out of that cloud down the steep abrupt full of gorges, scars, and ravines; and what was just now a picture of May-day peace became, on a sudden, a scene of whipped and creaming ripples; and the flashing on shore of the glass of shaken window-casements through spiral spirtings of reddish dust; hands aloft on the various ships at anchor, hastily furling the canvas that had been loosed to hang idly to the sun; flags, quite recently languid as streaks of paint, now pulling fiercely at their halliards; and Malay fishing-boats, darting across the bay in a gem-like glittering of water sliced out by their sharp stems and slung to the strong wind.

Under small sail we stormed out toward the ocean, with a desperate screaming of wind in the rigging; but there was no sea, for the gale was off the land; and after passing some noble and enchanting bays on whose shores the breakers as tall as our ship flung their resounding Atlantic thunder, whilst behind stood ranges of mountains putting a quality of solemn magnificence into the cheerful yellow clothing of the sunshine, with here and there a small house of an almond whiteness against the leaves of the silver trees and sundry rich growths thereabouts, in a moment we ran sheer out of the gale into a light wind, blowing from the north-west.

I don't say we were astonished, since somewhile before reaching the calm part we could see it clearly defined by the line where the froth and angry blueness and the fiery agitation of the wind ended. Still, it was impossible not to feel surprised as the ship slipped out of the enraged and yelling belt into a peaceful sea and a weak new wind which obliged us to handle the braces and make sail.

Here happened an extraordinary thing.

As we passed Green Point, where the
weather was placid and the strife waged in
the bay no longer to be seen, a large ship of
six hundred tons, that we supposed was to
call at Cape Town, passed us, her yards
braced up and all plain sail set. She had
some soldiers aboard, showed several guns,
had the English colours flying and offered
a very brave and handsome show, being
sheathed with copper that glowed ruddy to
the soft laving of the glass-bright swell, and
her canvas had the hue of the cotton cloths
which the Spaniards of the South American
main used to spread, and which in these days
form a distinguishing mark of the Yankee
ships. Having not the least suspicion of the
turmoil that awaited her round Mouille Point,
she slipped along jauntily, ready to make
a free wind of the breeze then blowing. But
all on a sudden, on opening the bay, she met
the whole strength of the fierce south-easter.
Down she lay to it, all aback—stopped dead.

Her ports being open, I feared if she were not promptly recovered, she must founder. They might let go the halliards, but the yards being jammed would not travel. It swept the heart into the throat to witness this thing! We brought our ship to the wind to render help with our boats; but happily her mizzen topmast broke, and immediately after, her main topgallant-mast snapped short off, close to the cross-trees; then—though it must have been wild work on those sloping decks—they managed to bring the main and topsail yards square; whereupon she paid off, righting as her head swung from the gale, and with lightened hearts, as may be supposed, they went to work to let go and clew up and haul down, whilst you saw how severe was the need of the pumps they had manned, by the bright streams of water which sluiced from her sides.

It was a cruel thing to witness, this sudden wrecking of the beauty of a truly stately ship, quietly swinging along over the mild heave of the swell, like a full-robed, handsome princess seized and torn by some loathsome monster, as we read of such matters in old romances. It was like the blighting breath of pestilence upon some fair form, converting into little better than a carcase what was just now a proud and regal shape, made beauteous by all that art could give her of apparel, and all that nature could impart of colour and lustre.

CHAPTER VI.

THE CAPTAIN SPEAKS AGAIN OF THE DEATH SHIP.

I HAD the first watch on the night of the day on which we left Table Bay: that is, from eight till midnight; and at two bells—nine o'clock—I was quietly pacing the deck, full of fancies struck into me by the beauty of the stars, among which, over the starboard yard-arms, hung the Southern Cross, shining purely, and by the mild glory of the moon that, though short of a day or two of being full, rained down a keen light that had a hint of rosiness in it, when Captain Skevington came out of the cabin, and stepping up to me stood a minute without speaking, gazing earnestly right around the sea-circle.

There was a small wind blowing and the

ship, under full sail, was softly pushing
southwards with a pleasant noise as of
the playing of fountains coming from the
direction of her bows.

"A quiet night, Fenton," said the captain,
presently.

"Aye, sir; quiet indeed. There's been a
small show of lightning away down in the
south-west. The wind hangs steady but a
little faint."

"The sort of night for meeting with
the Demon Ship, eh, Fenton?" cried he,
with a laugh that did not sound perfectly
natural.

"There's no chance of such a meeting, I
fear, sir."

"You fear?"

"Well," I exclaimed, struck by his quick
catching up of me, "I mean that as the
Demon Ship, as you term her, is one of the
wonders of the world, the seeing of her
would be a mighty experience—something

big enough in that way to keep a man talking about it all his life."

"God avert such a meeting!" said he, lifting his hat, and turning up his face to the stars.

I suppose, thought I, that our drawing close to the seas in which the Phantom cruises has stirred up his superstitious fears afresh.

" Did you speak to any one at Cape Town about Vanderdecken, sir?" said I.

"No," he answered. "I had got my belly-full from the master of the snow. What is there to ask?"

" Whether others have lately sighted the ship."

"Why, yes, I might have inquired, certainly, but it didn't enter my head. Tell ye what, though, Fenton, do you remember our chat t'other day about bodies being endevilled after they pass an age when by the laws of great Nature they should die?"

" Perfectly well, sir."

" Now," continued he, " I was in company a few nights since where there was one Cornelius Meyer present, a person ninety-one years old, but surprisingly sound in all his faculties, his sight piercing, his hearing keen, memory tenacious, and so forth. He was a Dutch Jew, but his patriotism was coloured by the hue of the flag flying at Cape Castle : I mean he would take the King of Great Britain and the States-General as they came. When he left we talked of him, and this led us to argue about old age. One gentleman said he did not know but that it was possible for a man to live to a hundred-and-fifty, and said there were instances of it. I replied, ' Not out of the Bible,' where the reckoning was not ours. He answered, 'Yes, out of the Bible;' and going to a bookshelf, pulled down a volume, and read a score of names of men with their ages attached. I looked at the

F

book and saw it was honestly written, and
being struck by this collection of extraordinary examples, begged the gentleman's
son, who was present, to copy the list out
for me, which he was so obliging as to do. I
have it in my pocket," said he, and he
pulled out a sheet of paper, and then going
to the hatch called to the boy to bring a
lamp on deck.

This was done, the lamp put on the sky-
light, and putting the paper close to it, the
captain read as follows : " Thomas Parr, of
Shropshire, died Nov. 16, 1635, aged one
hundred and fifty-two ; Henry Jenkins, of
Yorkshire, died Dec. 8, 1670, aged one
hundred and sixty-nine ; James Sands, of
Staffordshire, died 1770, aged one hundred
and forty ; Louisa Truxo, a negress in South
America, was living in 1780, and her age
was then one hundred and seventy-five."

I burst into a laugh. He smiled too, and
said, " Here in this list are thirty-one names,

the highest being that negress, and the
lowest one, Susannah Hilliar, of Piddington,
Northamptonshire, who died February 19th,
1781, aged one hundred. The young gentleman who copied them said they were all
honestly vouched for, and wrote down a list
of the authorities, which," said he, peering
and bringing the paper closer to his eyes,
"consist of 'Fuller's Worthies,' 'Philosophical
Transactions,' 'Derham's Physico-Theology,'
several newspapers, such as the 'Morning
Post,' 'Daily Advertiser,' 'London Chronicle,'
and a number of inscriptions."

I could have been tolerably sarcastic, I
daresay, when he mentioned the authority
of the newpapers, always understanding that
those sheets flourish mainly on lies, and I
should have laughed again had I not been re-
strained by the sense that Captain Skevington
was clearly "bitten" on this subject, actually
worried by it, indeed, to such lengths, that
if he did not mind his eye it might presently

push into a delusion, and earn him the dis-
concerting reputation of being a madman ; so
I thought I would talk gravely, and said,
" May I ask, sir, why you should have been
at the pains to collect that evidence in your
hand about old age ?"

" A mere humour," said he, lightly, putting
the paper away, " though I don't mind owning it would prodigiously gratify me if I
could be the instrument of proving that men
can overstep the bounds of natural life by as
many years again, and yet possess their own
souls and be as true to their original as they
were when hearty young fellows flushed with
the summer colours of life."

Some fine rhymes coming into my head, I
exclaimed, " Cowley has settled that point, I
think, when he says :—

> ' To things immortal time can do no wrong,
> And that which never is to die for ever must be
> young.'

" A noble fancy indeed !" cried the captain.
He reflected a little, and said, " It would

make a great noise among sailors, and perhaps all men, to prove that the mariners who
man the Death Ship are not ghosts and
phantoms as has been surmised, but survivors
of a crew, men who have outlived their
fellows, and are now extremely ancient, as
these and scores of others who have passed
away unnoticed have been," said he, touching
his pocket where the paper was.

"When, sir, did Vanderdecken sail from
Batavia?" I asked.

"I have always understood about the year
1650," he replied.

"Then," said I, calculating, "suppose the
average age of the crew to have been thirty
when the Curse was uttered—we'll name that
figure for the sake of argument—in the
present year of our Lord they will have
attained the age of hard upon one hundred
and eighty."

"Well?" said he, inquiringly, as though
there was yet food for argument.

I shook my head.

"Then," he cried, with heat, "they are endevilled, for it must be one of two things. They can't be dead men as the corpse in the grave is dead."

"One could only judge by seeing with one's eyes," said I.

"I hope that won't happen," he exclaimed, taking a hasty turn; "though I don't know —I don't know! A something here," pressing his brow, "weighs down upon me like a warning. I have struggled to get rid of the fancy; but our being chased by the Dutchman shows that we did not meet that Plymouth snow for nothing; and, by the thunder of Heaven, Fenton, I fear—I fear our next bout will be with the Spectre."

His manner, his words, a gleam in his eye, to which the lantern lent no sparkle, sent a tremor through me. He caused me to fear him for a minute as one that talked with certainty of futurity through stress of pro-

phetic craze.   The yellow beams of the
lantern dispersed a narrow circle of lustre,
and in it our figures showed black, each with
two shadows swaying at his feet from the
commingling of the lamplight and the
moonshine.   The soft air stirred in the
rigging like the rustle of the pinions of
invisible night-birds on the wing ; all was
silent and in darkness along the decks, save
where stood the figure of the helmsman
just before the little round-house, outlined by
the flames of the binnacle lamp ; the stillness,
unbroken to the farthest corners of the
mighty plain of ocean, seemed as though
it were some mysterious spell wrought by the
stars, so high it went, even—so one might
say—as a sensible presence to the busy,
trembling faces of those silver worlds.

In all men, even in the dullest, there is a
vein of imagination ; whilst, like an artery, it
holds sound, all is well.   But sometimes it
breaks, God knows how, for the most part,

and then what is in it floods the intelligence
often to the drowning of it, as the bursting of
a vessel of the body within sickens or kills
with hemorrhage. I considered some such
idea as this to be applicable to Captain
Skevington.   Here was apparently a plain,
sturdy sailor, qualified to the life for such talk
as concerns ships, weather, ladings and the
like ; yet it was certain he was exceedingly
superstitious, believing in such a Devil as the
ancient monks figured forth, also in the possession of dead bodies by demons who caused
them to move and act as though operated
upon by the souls they came from their
mothers with, with a vast deal of other piti-
ful fancies ; and now, through our unhappy
meeting with that miserable snow, he had
let his mind run on the Phantom Ship so
vehemently that he was not only cocksure
we should meet the Spectre, but had reasoned
the whole fabric and manning of her out on
two issues ; either that her hands were sur-

vivors of her original crew, persons who had
cheated Nature by living to an age the like
of which had not been heard of since the
days of Moses and the prophets, beings who,

> Like a lamp would live to the last wink
> And crawl upon the utmost verge of life ;

or that they were mariners who, having
arrived at the years when they would have
died but for being cursed, had been seized
upon by the Devil, quickened by him, and
set a-going with their death-hour aspects
upon them.

These reflections occupied my mind after
he had left me, and I don't mind confessing
that what with my own belief in the Death
Ship, coupled with the captain's notions and
the fancies they raised in me, along with the
melancholy vagueness of the deep, hazy with
moonshine, the stillness, and the sense of our
drawing near to where the Spectre was
chiefly to be met, I became so uneasy that I
contrived to spend the rest of my watch on

deck within a few paces of the wheel, often
addressing the helmsman for the sake of
hearing his voice; and I tell you I was mighty
pleased when midnight came round at last,
so that I could go below and dispatch the
mate to a scene in which his heavy mind
would witness nothing but water and sky,
and a breeze much too faint to be profitable.

CHAPTER VII.

I CONVERSE WITH THE SHIP'S CARPENTER ABOUT THE DEATH SHIP.

AND now for six days it veritably seemed as if we were to be transformed into the marine phantom that, unsubstantial as she might be, yet lay with the heaviness of lead upon Captain Skevington ; for, being on the parallel of Agulhas, a little to the south of that latitude, and in about sixteen degrees west longitude, it came on to blow fresh from the south-east, hardening after twenty-four hours into a whole gale with frequent and violent guns, and a veering of it easterly ; and this continued, with a lull of an hour or two's duration, for six days, as I have said. 'Twas a taste of Cape weather strong enough

to last a man a lifetime. The sea lay
shrouded to within a musket-shot by a
vapour of slatish hue that looked to stand
motionless, and past the walls and along
the roof of this wild, dismal, cloud-formed
chamber, with its floor of vaults and frothing
brows, the wind swept raving, raising a
terrible lead-coloured sea, with heads which
seemed to rear to the height of our maintop,
where they broke, and boiled like a cauldron
with foam, great masses of which the hands
of the gale caught up and hurled, so that the
lashing of the spray was often like a blinding
snowstorm, but so smarting that the wind
was as if charged with javelins.

Look upon the chart and you will see that
for measureless leagues there is in these
waters no land to hinder the run of the
surges. Hence, when a fierce gale comes on
from the east, south or west, the seas which
rise are prodigious beyond such language as
I have at command to express. We lay-to

under a storm staysail with topgallant-masts struck, yards on deck and the lower yards stowed on the rail, the hatches battened down and everything as snug as good seamanship could provide. Our decks were constantly full of water; by one great sea that fell over into the waist there were drowned no less than six of the sheep we had taken in at the Cape, with a hog and many fowls; the carpenter's leg was broken by a fall, and an able seaman was deeply gashed in the face by being thrown against a scuttle-butt; 'twas impossible to get any food cooked, and throughout that week we subsisted on biscuit, cheese and such dry and lean fare as did not need dressing. In short, I could fill a chapter with our sufferings and anxieties during that period.

I had supposed that when brought face to face with the stern harsh prose of such weather as this, the mournful, romantic stuff that filled the captain's head would have been clean blown out of it; but no! he repeatedly said to me, and I believe on more than one occasion to Mr. Hall, that he considered this weather as part of the ill-luck that was bound to come to us from our having spoken a vessel that had been passed within hailing distance by the Phantom Ship.

On the fifth morning of the gale, the pair of us being in the cabin, he informed me that a man named Cobwebb, who was at the helm the night before, had told him that some of the crew were for putting this foul storm down to one Mulder, or some such name, who was a Russian Finn, a sober, excellent seaman, and one of the only two foreigners in our forecastle; that to neutralise any magical influence he might possess, a horse shoe had been nailed to the foremast and the mainmast pierced and scored with a black-handled knife. He smiled at these superstitions but did not seem to suspect that his own, as being received by a man of thought and tolerable education, might by many be deemed much more worthy of ridicule.

But on the sixth day the gale broke, leaving our ship considerably strained, by which time, in spite of the current and the send of the sea, we had contrived to make forty miles of southing and easting, owing to our pertinacity in making sail and stretching away on a board at every lull.

It was shortly after this, on the Tuesday following the Friday on which the gale ended, that, it being my watch on deck from eight o'clock in the evening till midnight, I carried my pipe, an hour before my turn arrived, into the carpenter's cabin, which he shared with the boatswain, to give the poor fellow a bit of my company, for his broken leg kept him motionless. It was the second dog-watch, as we term the time, 'twixt six and eight o'clock, at sea, the evening indifferently fine, the wind over the starboard quarter, a quiet breeze, the ocean heaving in a lazy swell from the south, and the ship pushing forward at five knots an hour under fore and main-royals. The carpenter lay in a bunk, wearing a haggard face, and grizzly for lack of the razor. He was a very sensible, sober man, a good artificer, and had served under Lord Howe in the fleet equipped for the relief of Gibraltar, besides having seen a deal of cruising work in earlier times.

He was much obliged by my looking in upon him, and we speedily fell to yarning ; he lighted a pipe, and I smoked likewise, whilst I sat upon his chest, taking in with a half-look round, such details as a rude sketch of the bo's'n's wife nailed to the bulkhead, the slush lamp swinging its dingy smoking flame to a cracked piece of looking-glass over against the carpenter's bed, an ancient horny copy of the Bible, with type pretty nigh as big as the letters of our ship's name, a bit of a shelf wherefrom there forked out the stems of some clay pipes, with other

humble furniture such as a sailor is used
to carry to sea with him.

After a little, the carpenter, whose name
was Matthews, says to me, "I beg pardon,
sir, but there's some talk going about among
the men concerning the old Dutchman that
was cursed last century. My mate, Joe
Marner, told me that Jimmy—meaning the
cabin-boy—was telling some of the crew this
morning, that he heard the captain say the
Dutchman's been sighted."

"By anyone aboard us?" I asked.

"Mebbe, sir, but I didn't understand
that."

Now, as every hour was carrying us
further to the eastward of the Cape, away
from the Phantom's cruising-ground, and as,
moreover, the leaving gossip to make its own
way would surely in the end prove more
terrifying to the nervous and superstitious on
board than speaking the truth, I resolved to
tell Matthews how the matter stood, and with

that, acquainted him with what the master of
the snow had told Captain Skevington. He
looked very grave, and withdrew his pipe
from his lips, and I noticed he did not offer
to light the tobacco afresh.

" I'm sorry to hear this, sir," says he.

" But," said I, " what has the Lovely
Nancy's meeting with the Dutchman got to
do with us?"

"Only this, sir," he exclaimed, with his
face yet more clouded, and speaking in a low
voice, as one might in a sacred building, " I
never yet knew or heard of a ship reporting
to another of having met the Dutchman
without that other a-meeting of the Ghost too
afore she ended her voyage."

" If that be so," I cried, not liking to hear
this, for Matthews had been to sea for thirty-
five years, and he now spoke with too much
emotion not to affect me, "for God's sake
don't make your thoughts known to the crew,
and least of all to the captain, who is already

so uneasy on this head that when he mentions it he talks as if his mind were adrift."

"Mr. Fenton," said the carpenter, "I never yet knew or heard of a ship reporting to another of having met the Dutchman, without that other meeting the Ghost too afore she's ended her voyage," and thus speaking he smote his bed heavily with his fist.

I was startled by the emphasis his repeating his former words gave to the assurance, and smoked in silence. He put down his pipe and lay awhile looking at me as though turning some matters over in his mind. The swing of the flame, burning from the spout of the lamp put various expressions, wrought by the fluctuating shadows, into his sick face, and it was this perhaps that caused his words to possess a power I could not feign to you by any art of my pen. He asked me if I had ever seen the Dutchman, and on my answering "No," he said that the usual notion among sailors was that there is but one vessel sailing the seas with the curse of Heaven upon her, but that that was a mistake, as it was an error in the same way to suppose that this ocean from Agulhas round to the Mozambique was the only place in which the Phantom was to be met.

"There's a ship," said he, "after the pattern of this here Dutchman, to be found in the Baltic. She always brings heavy weather, and there's small chance afterwards for any craft that sights her."

"I've been trading in the Baltic for five years without ever hearing that," said I.

"But it's true all the same, Mr. Fenton; you ask about it, sir, when you get back, and then you'll see. There's another vessel, of the same pattern, that's to be met down in the mouth of the Channel, 'twixt Ushant and the Scillies, and thereabouts. A man I know, called Jimmy Robbins, saw her, and told me the yarn. He was in a ship bound home from the Spice Islands; they were in soundings, and heading round for the Channel; it was the morning watch, just about dawn, weather slightly thickish; suddenly a vessel comes heaving out of the smother from God knows where! Jim Robbins was coiling down a rope alongside the mate, who, on seeing the vessel, screams out shrill, like a woman, and falls flat in a swound; Jim, looking, saw it was the Channel Death Ship, a large pink, manned by skeletons, with a skull for a figure-head, and a skeleton captain leaning against the mast, watching the running of the sand in an hour-glass he held. She was seen by twelve others, besides Jim and the mate, who nearly died of the fright. And the consequence of meeting her was, that the ship Jim Robbins was in was cast away on the following night on the French coast, down Saint Brihos way, and thirty-three souls perished."

The gravity with which he related this, and his evident keen belief in these and the like superstitions, now rendered the conversation somewhat diverting; for, as I have elsewhere said, though I never questioned the existence of the one spectral ship, in a belief in which all mariners are united, holding that the deep, which is full of drowned men, hath its spirits and its apparitions equally with the land, yet when it came to such crude mad fancies as a vessel manned by skeletons, why, of course, there was nothing for it but to laugh, which I did, heartily enough, though in my sleeve, for seamen are a sensitive people, easily afronted, more especially in any article of their faith. However, he succeeded, before I left him, in exciting a fresh uneasiness in me by asseverating, in a most melancholy voice, and with a very dismal face, that our having spoken with the snow that had sighted the Dutchman was certain to be followed by misfortune; and these being amongst the last words he exchanged with me before I left his cabin, I naturally carried away with me on deck the damping and desponding impression of his posture and appearance as he uttered them, which were those of a man grieved, bewildered, and greatly alarmed.

CHAPTER VIII.

A TRAGICAL DEATH.

FOR some time after I had relieved the deck, as it is termed, that is to say, after the mate had gone below and left me in charge, I had the company of the captain, who seemed restless and troubled, often quitting my side as we paced, to go to the rail and view the horizon, with the air of a man perturbed by expectation. I need not tell you that I did not breathe a word to him respecting my talk with the carpenter, not even to the extent of saying how fancies about the Dutchman were flying about among the crew, for this subject he was in no state of mind to be brought into.

The moon was rising a little before he joined me, and we stood in silence watching her. She jutted up a very sickly faint red, that brightened but a little after she lifted her lower limb clear of the horizon, and when we had the full of her plain we perceived her strangely distorted by the atmosphere of the shape—if shape it can be called—of a rotten orange that has been squeezed, or of a turtle's egg lightly pressed ; she was more like a blood-coloured jelly distilled by the sky, ugly and even affrighting, than the sweet ice-cold planet that empearls the world at night, and whose delicate silver the lover delights to behold in his sweetheart's eyes. But she grew more shapely as she soared, though holding a dusky blush for a much longer time than ever I had noticed in her when rising off the mid-African main ; and her wake, broken by the small, black curl of the breeze, hung in broken indissoluble lumps of feverish light, like coagulated gore that had dropped from the wound she looked to be in the dark sky.

There was a faintness in the heavens that closed out the sparkles of the farther stars, and but a few, and those only of the greatest magnitude, were visible, shining in several colours, such as dim pink and green and wan crystal; all which, together with one or two of them above our mastheads, dimly glittering amidst feeble rings, made the whole appearance of the night amazing and even ghastly enough to excite a feeling of awe in the attention it compelled. The captain spoke not a word whilst the moon slowly floated into the dusk, and then fetching a deep breath, he said—

" Well, thank God, if she don't grow round it's because of the shadow on her. Keep a bright look-out, Mr. Fenton, and hold the ship to her course. Should the wind fail call me—and call me too if it should head us."

With which he walked quietly to the hatch, stood there a moment or two with his hand upon it and his face looking up as though he studied the trim of the yards, and then disappeared.

My talk with the carpenter and the behaviour of the captain bred in me a sense as of something solemn and momentous informing the hours. I reasoned with myself, I struggled with the inexplicable oppression that weighed down my spirits, but it would not do. I asked myself, "Why should the cheap, illiterate fears of such a man as the carpenter affect me? Why should I find the secret of my soul's depression in the superstitions of Captain Skevington, whose arguments as to the endevilment of the dead exhibited a decay of his intellect on one side, as phthisis consumes one lung, leaving the other sound enough for a man to go on living with?" And I recited these comfortable lines of the poet :—

> "Learn though mishap may cross our ways,
>   It is not ours to reckon when."

Yet in vain. There was an intelligence of

my spirits that was not to be soothed, and I found myself treading about the deck, stepping lightly, as a man might who walks upon ground under which the dead lie, whilst I felt so much worried, down to the very bottom of my heart, that had some great sorrow just befallen me I could not have been sadder.

As the night wore on the moon gathered her wonted hue and shape, though her refulgence was small, for the air thickened. Indeed, at half-past ten all the lights of Heaven, saving the moon, had been put out by a mist, the texture of which was illustrated by the only luminary the sky contained, around whose pale expiring disc there was now a great halo, with something of the character of a lunar rainbow in the very delicate, barely determinable tinctures, which made a sort of shadowy prism of it, more like what one would dream of than see. The ocean lay very black, there was no power in the moon to cast a wake, the breathings of

the wind rippled the water and caused a scin-
tillation of the spangles of the phosphorus or
sea-fire, the weight of the lower sails kept
them hanging up and down, and what motion
the ship had was from the swelling of the
light canvas that rose very pale and ghostly
into the gloom.

I had gone to the taffrail and was staring
there away into the dark, whither our short
wake streamed in a sort of smouldering
cloudiness with particles of fire in it, conceiving that the wind was failing, and waiting
to make sure before reporting to the captain,
when I was startled by the report of a
musket or some small arm that broke upon
my ear with a muffled sound, so that whence
it came I could not conceive. Yet, for some
minutes I felt so persuaded the noise had
been seawards that, spite of there having
been no flash, I stood peering hard into the
dark, first one side then the other, far as the
sails would suffer me.

Then, but all very quickly, concluding that the explosion had happened aboard and might betoken mischief, I ran along the deck where, close against the wheel, I found a number of seamen talking hurriedly and in alarmed voices. I called out to know what that noise had been. None knew. One said it had come from the sea, another that there had been a small explosion in the hold, and a third was giving his opinion, when at that instant a figure darted out of the companion hatch, clothed in his shirt and drawers, and cried out, " Mr. Fenton ! Mr. Fenton ! For God's sake, where are you ?"

I recognized the voice of Mr. Hall, and bawled back, " Here, sir !" and ran to him. He grasped my arm. " The captain has shot himself !" he exclaimed.

" Where is he ?" said I.

" In his cabin," he answered.

We rushed down together. The great cabin, where we messed, was in darkness, but a light shone in the captain's berth. The door was open, and gently swung with the motion of the ship. I pushed in, but instantly recoiled with horror, for, right athwart the deck lay the body of Captain Skevington, with the top of his head blown away. It needed but one glance to know that he had done this thing with his own hand. He had fired the piece with his foot by a string attached to the trigger, standing upright with his brow bent to the muzzle, for the bight of the string was round his shoe, and he had fallen sideways, grasping the barrel.

The sight froze me to the marrow. Had I killed him by accident with my own hand I could not have trembled more. But this exquisite distress was short-lived. It was only needful to look at his head to discover how fruitless would be the task of examining him for any signs of life. Some of the seamen who heard Mr. Hall cry out to me about this thing had followed us below, forgetting their place in the consternation roused in them, and stood in the doorway faintly groaning and muttering exclamations of pity. Mr. Hall bid a couple of them raise the body and lay it in its bunk and cover it with a sheet, and others he sent for water and a swab wherewith to cleanse the place.

"You had better go on deck again, Fenton," says he to me; "the ship must be watched. I'll join you presently."

I was glad to withdraw; for albeit there was a ghastliness in the look of the night, the sea being black as ebony, though touched here and there with little sheets of fire, and stretching like a pall to its horizon that was drawing narrower and murkier around us minute after minute, with the wing-like shadow of vapour that was yet too thin to deserve the name of fog; though there was this ghastliness, I say, aided by the moon that was now little more than a dim, tar-

nished blotch of shapeless silver, wanly ringed
with an ashen cincture, yet the taste of the
faint breeze was as helpful to my spirits as
a dram of generous cordial after the atmosphere of the cabin in which I had beheld
the remains of Captain Skevington.

CHAPTER IX.

MR. HALL HARANGUES THE CREW.

THE news had spread quickly; the watch below had roused out and most of the men were on deck, and they moved about in groups striving to find out all about the suicide. The death of a captain of a ship at sea is sure always to fill the crew with uneasiness; a sense of uncertainty is excited, and then again there is that darkening of the spirits which the shadow of death particularly causes among a slender community who have been for months associated as a family, and amid whom, every man's face, speech, and manner are, maybe, more familiar than his own brother's or father's.

Yet of all the souls on board I suspect I

felt the captain's self-murder most sorely, for owing to there being in my mind much more that was akin to his own moods than he could find in Mr. Hall, we had had many and long conversations together. Then there was the Death Ship for me to recall, with his thoughts on it and his conviction that evil was sure to follow his boarding the Plymouth snow. Moreover, I was the last with whom he had exchanged words that night, and in his manner of quitting me, after looking at the moon, there was positively nothing that even my startled and imaginative mind could witness to indicate the intention that had destroyed him.

Presently Mr. Hall arrived on deck fully dressed, and stepping over to where I stood in deep thought, exclaimed, " Did you have a suspicion that the captain designed this fearful act ?"

" No, not a shadow of a suspicion," I answered.

" 'Tis enough to make one believe he was not far out when he talked of the ill-luck he expected from speaking a craft that had sighted Vanderdecken," said he, very uneasily, which made me see how strong was the blow his nerves had received ; and running his eyes restlessly over the water here and there, as I might tell by the dim sparkle the faint moon-haze kindled in them. " Oh, but," he continued, as if dashing aside his fancies, " the mere circumstance of his being so superstitious ought to explain the act. I have often thought there was a vein of madness in him."

" I never questioned that," I replied.

" 'Tis an ugly-looking night," said he, with a little tremble running through him, " there is some menace of foul weather. We shall lose this faint air presently." He shivered again and said, " Such a sight as that below is enough to make a Hell of a night of midsummer beauty ! It is the suddenness of it that seizes upon the imagination Why, d'ye know, Fenton, I'd give a handful of guineas, poor as I am, for a rousing gale —anything to blow my mind to its bearings, for here's a sort of business," looking aloft, " that's fit to suffocate the heart in your breast."

Such words in so plain and literal a man made me perceive how violently he had been wrenched. I begged his leave to go below and fetch him a glass of liquor.

" No, no," said he, "not yet, anyhow. I must speak to those fellows there."

Saying which he walked a little distance forward, calling for the boatswain.

On that officer answering, he said, " Are all hands on deck ?"

" I believe most of the crew are on deck, sir," replied the boatswain.

" Pipe all hands," said Mr. Hall.

The clear keen whistling rose shrill to the sails and made as blythe a sound as could

have been devised for the cheering of us up.
The men gathered quickly, some lanthorns
were fetched, and in the light of them stood
the crew near to the round-house. A strange
sight it was; the shining went no higher than
half-way up the mainsail that hung steady
with its own weight, and as much of it as was
thus illuminated showed like cloth of gold
pale in the dusk; above was mere shadow,
the round-top like a drop of ink upon the
face of the darkness, the sails of so weak a
hue they seemed as though in the act of
dissolving and vanishing away; the crowd of
faces were all pale and their eyes full of
gleaming; the shadows crawled at our feet,
and, with the total concealment of the moon
at this time, a deeper shade fell upon the sea
and our ship, and the delicate rippling of the
water alongside seemed to stir upon our ears
in a tinkling as from out of the middle air.

Mr. Hall made a brief speech. He ex-
plained to the men how, on hearing the

report of a musket, he had sprung from his
bed, and perceiving powder-smoke leaking
through the openings in the door of the
captain's cabin, through which some rays
of light streamed, he entered, and seeing
the body of the captain, and the horrid condition of the head, was filled with a panic
and rushed on deck. That the master had
shot himself was certain, but there was no
help for what had happened. The command of the ship fell upon him; but it was
for them to say whether he should navigate
the ship to her destination, or carry her back
to Table Bay, where a fresh commander
could be obtained.

He was very well liked on board, being
an excellent seaman; and the crew on hearing this, immediately answered that they
wanted no better master to sail under than
he, and that, indeed, they would not consent
to a change; but having said this with a
heartiness that pleased me, for I liked Mr.

Hall greatly myself, and was extremely glad
to find the crew so well disposed, they fell
into an awkward silence, broken after a little
by some hoarse whisperings.

"What now?" says Mr. Hall.

"Why, sir," answers the boatswain, re-
spectfully, "it's this with the men: there's
a notion among us that that there Plymouth
snow has brought ill-luck to the ship, one
bad specimen of which has just happened;
and the feeling is that we had better return
to Table Bay, so as to get the influence
worked out of the old barkey."

"How is that to be done?" says Mr. Hall,
coming easily into the matter, partly because
of his shaken nerves, and partly because of
the kindness he felt towards the hands for
the way they had received his address to
them.

Here there was another pause, and then
the boatswain, speaking somewhat shyly,
said, "The carpenter, who's heard tell more

about the Phantom Ship and the spell she lays on vessels than all hands of us put together, says that the only way to work out of a ship's timbers the ill-luck that's been put into them by what's magical and hellish, is for a minister of religion to come aboard, call all hands to prayer, and ask of the Lord a blessing on the ship. He says there's no other way of purifying of her."

"Can't we pray ourselves for a blessing?" says Mr. Hall.

The boatswain not quickly answering, a sailor says, "It needs a man who knows how to pray — who's acquainted with the right sort of words to use."

"Aye," cried another, "and whose calling is religion."

Mr. Hall half-turned, as if he would address me, then checking himself, he said, "Well, my lads, there's no wind now, and small promise of any. Suppose we let this matter rest till to-morrow morning; Mr.

Fenton and I will talk it over, and you forward can turn it about in your minds. I believe we shall be easier when the captain's buried and the sun's up, and then we might agree it would be a pity to put back after the tough job we've had to get where we are. But lest you should still be all of one mind on this matter in the morning, we'll keep the ship, should wind come, under small sail, so as to make no headway worth speaking of during the night. Is that to your fancy, men ?"

They all said it was, and thereupon went forward, but I noticed that those who were off duty did not offer to go below ; they joined the watch on the forecastle, and I could hear them in earnest talk, their voices trembling through the stillness like the humming of a congregation in church following the parson's reading.

Mr. Hall came to my side and we walked the deck.

" I am sorry the men have got that notion of this ship being under a spell," said he. " This is no sweet time of the year in these seas ; to put back will, I daresay, be only to anger the weather that's now quiet enough, and there's always the risk of falling into Dutch hands."

I told him of my talk with the carpenter, and said that I could not be surprised the crew were alarmed, for the old fellow had the Devil's own knack of putting his fancies in an alarming way.

" I laughed at some of his fancies," said I, " but I don't mind owning that I quitted his cabin so dulled in my spirits by his talk, that I might have come from a death-bed for all the heart there was in me."

" Well, things must take their chance," said Mr. Hall. " I'll speak to the carpenter myself in the morning, and afterwards to the men ; and if they are still wishful that the ship should return to Table Bay we'll sail her

there.   Tis all one to me   I'd liefer have a
new captain over me than be one."

We continued until five bells to walk to
and fro the deck, talking about the captain's
suicide, the strangeness of it as following his
belief that ill-luck had come to the ship from
the Plymouth vessel, with other such matters
as would be suggested by our situation and
the tragedy in the cabin ; and Mr. Hall then
said he would go below for a glass of rum ;
but he refused to lie down—though I offered
to stand an hour of his watch, that is from
midnight till one o'clock — for he said he
should not be able to sleep.

Most of the crew continued to hang about
the forecastle, which rescued the deck from
the extreme loneliness I had found in it ere
the report of the fatal musket startled all
hands into wakefulness and movement. The
lanthorns had been carried away and the ship
was plunged in darkness. There still blew a
very light air, so gentle that you needed to

wet your finger and hold it up to feel it. From the darkness aloft fell the delicate sounds of the higher canvas softly drumming the masts to the very slight rolling of the ship. I went to the binnacle and found that the vessel was heading her course, and then stepped to the rail, upon which I set my elbows, leaning my chin in my hands, and in that posture fell a-thinking.

CHAPTER X.

Now I might have stood thus for ten minutes, when I was awakened from my dream by an eager feverish muttering of voices forward, and on a sudden the harsh notes of a seaman belonging to my watch cried out, " D'ye see that sail, right broad a-beam, sir?"

I sprang from my leaning posture, and peered, but my eyes were heavy ; the night was dark, and whilst I stared several of the sailors came hurriedly aft to where I stood, and said, all speaking together, " There— see her, sir? Look yonder, Mr. Fenton!" and their arms, to a man, shot out to point, as if every one levelled a pistol.

Though I could not immediately make out the object, I was not surprised by the consternation the sailors were in ; for, such was the mood and temper of the whole company, that not the most familiar and prosaic craft that floats on the ocean could have broken through the obscurity of the night upon their gaze without tickling their superstitious instincts, till the very hair of their heads crawled to the inward motions. In a few moments, sure enough, I made out the loom of what looked a large ship, out on the starboard beam. As well as I could distinguish she was close hauled, and so standing as to pass under our stern. She made a sort of faintness upon the sea and sky where she was : nothing more. And even to be sure of her, it was necessary to look a little on one side or the other of her ; for if you gazed full she went out, as a dim distant light at sea does, thus viewed.

"She may be an enemy !" I cried.

" There should be no lack of Dutch or even French hereabouts. Quick, lads, to stations. Send the boatswain here."

I ran to the companion hatch and called loudly to Mr. Hall. He had fallen asleep on a locker, and came running in a blind sort of way to the foot of the ladder, shouting out, "What is it? What is it?" I answered that there was a large ship heading directly for us, whereupon he was instantly wide awake, and sprang up the ladder, crying, "Where away? Where away?"

If there was any wind I could feel none. Yet some kind of draught there must have been, for the ship out in the darkness held a brave luff, which proved her under command. We, on the other hand, rested upon the liquid ebony of the ocean with square yards, the mizzen furled, the starboard clew of the mainsail hoisted, and the greater number of our staysails down. Whilst Mr. Hall stared in the direction of the ship the boatswain arrived for orders. The mate turned smartly to me, and said, "We must make ready, and take our chance. Bo's'n, pipe to quarters, and Mr. Fenton, see all clear."

For the second time in my watch the boatswain's pipe shrilled clear to the canvas, from whose stretched, still folds, the sounds broke away in ghostly echoes. We were not a man-of-war, had no drums, and to martial duties we could but address ourselves clumsily. But all felt that there might be a great danger in the pale shadow yonder that had seemed to ooze out upon our eyes from the darkness as strangely as a cloud shapes itself upon a mountain-top.

So we tumbled about quickly and wildly enough, got our little batteries clear, put on the hatch-gratings and tarpaulins, opened the magazine, lighted the matches, provided the guns with spare breeches and tackles, and stood ready for whatever was to come. All this we contrived with the aid of one or two

lanterns, very secretly moved about, as Mr.
Hall did not wish us to be seen making
ready; but the want of light delayed us,
and, by the time we were fully prepared,
the strange ship had insensibly floated down
to about three-quarters-of-a-mile upon our
starboard quarter.

At that distance it was too black to enable
us to make anything of her, but we com-
forted ourselves by observing that she did
not offer to alter her course, whence we
might reasonably hope that she was a peaceful trader like ourselves. She showed no
lights—her sails were all that was visible of
her, owing to the hue they put into the darkness over her hull. It was a time of heavy
trial to our patience. Our ship had come to
a dead stand, as it was easy to discover by
looking over the side, where the small, pale
puffs of phosphoric radiance that flashed
under water at the depth of a man's hand
from our vessel's strakes whenever she

rolled, no matter how daintily, to the swell, hung glimmering for a space in the selfsame spot where they were discharged. Nor was there the least sound of water in motion under our counter, unless it were the gurgling, drowning sobbing you hear there on a still night, when the stern stoops to the drop of the fold, and raises that strange, hollow noise of washing all about the rudder.

" I would to mercy a breeze would come if only to resolve her!" said Mr. Hall to me in a low voice. " There's but little fun to be got out of this sort of waiting. At this rate we must keep the men at their stations till daylight to find out what she is. Pleasant if she should prove some lump of a Dutch man-of-war! She shows uncommonly large, don't you think, Fenton?"

" So do we to her, I dare say, in this obscurity," I replied. " But I doubt that she's a man-of-war. I've been watching her closely and have never once caught sight of the least gleam of a light aboard her."

" Maybe the officer of the watch and the look-out are sound asleep," said he, with a slight and not very merry laugh ; " and if she's steered on her quarter-deck she'll be too deep-waisted perhaps for the helmsman to see us."

I heard him say this without closely heeding it, for my attention at that moment was attracted by what was unquestionably the enlargement of her pallid shadow ; sure proof that she had shifted her helm and was slowly coming round so as to head for us. Mr. Hall noticed this as soon as I.

" Ha !" he cried, "they mean to find out what we are, hey ? They've observed us at last. Does she bring an air with her that she's under control, or is it that she's lighter and taller than we ?"

It was beyond question because she was lighter and taller, and having been kept close-

hauled to the faint draught had made more
of it than we who carried it aft. Besides, we
were loaded down to our chain-plate bolts
with cargo, and the water and other stores
we had shipped at the Cape. Yet her
approach was so sluggish as to be impercep-
tible, and I would not like to say that our
gradual drawing together was not as much
due to the current which, off this coast, runs
strong to the westward, setting us, who were
deep, faster towards her than it set her from
us, as it was also owing to the strange attrac-
tion which brings becalmed vessels near to
each other—often indeed, to their having to
be towed clear by their boats.

Meanwhile, the utter silence on board the
stranger, the blackness in which her hull lay
hidden, the strangeness of her bracing-in her
yards to head up for us without any signal
being shown that she designed to fight us,
wrought such a fit of impatience in Mr. Hall,
that he swung his body from the backstay

he clutched in movements positively convulsive.

"Are they all dead aboard? On such a night as this one should be able to hear the least sound—the hauling taut of a tackle—the rasping of the wheel-ropes!"

"She surely doesn't hope to catch us napping?" said I.

"God knows!" cried the mate. "What would I give now for a bit of moon!"

"If it's to be a fight it'll have to be a shooting match for a spell, or wind must come quickly," said I. "But if she meant mischief wouldn't she head to pass under our stern, where she could rake us, rather than steer to come broadside on?"

Instead of responding, the mate sprang on to the bulwark-rail, and in tones such as only the practised and powerful lungs of a seaman can fling, roared out—

"Ho, the ship, ahoy!"

We listened with so fierce a strain of atten-

tion that the very beating of our hearts rung
in our ears ; but not a sound came across the
water.   Twice yet did Mr. Hall hail that
pallid fabric, shapeless as yet in the dark air,
but to no purpose.   On this there was much
whispering among the men clustered about
the guns.   Their voices came along in a
low, grumbling sound like the growling of
dogs, dulled by threats.

"Silence, fore and aft!" cried the mate.
"We don't know what she is — but we
know what we are! and, as Englishmen,
we surely have spirit enough for whatever
may come."

There was silence for some minutes after
these few words ; then the muttering broke
out afresh, but scattered, a group talking to
larboard, another on the forecastle, and so
forth.

Meanwhile the vessels, all insensibly, had
continued to draw closer and closer to each
other.   A small clarification of the atmos-

phere happening past the stranger, suffered a
dim disclosure of her canvas, whence I perceived that she had nothing set above her
topgallant-sails, though it was impossible to
see whether she carried royal-masts, or indeed
whether the yards belonging to those masts
were crossed on them. Her hull had now
also stolen out into a pitch-black shadow, and
after gazing at it with painful intentness for
some moments, I was extravagantly astonished to observe a kind of crawling and
flickering of light, resembling that which
burnt in the sea, stirring like glow-worms
along the vessel's side.

I was about to direct Mr. Hall's attention
to this thing, when he said in a subdued
voice, " Fenton, d'ye notice the faint shining
about her hull? What, in God's name, can it
be ?"

He had scarce uttered these words when a
sailor on the starboard side of our ship, whom
I recognised by the voice as one Ephraim

Jacobs, an elderly, sober, pious-minded seaman, cried out with a sort of scream in his .
notes—

"As I hope to be forgiven my sins for
Jesu's sake, yon's the ship that was curst
last century."

CHAPTER XI.

THE mere putting into words the suspicion that had been troubling all our minds made one man in action of the whole crew, like the firing of forty pieces of ordnance in the same instant. Whatever the sailors held they flung down, and, in a bound, came to the waist on the starboard side, where they stood, looking at the ship and making, amid that silence, the strangest noise that ever was heard with their deep and fearful breathing.

"Great thunder!" broke in one of them, presently, "d'ye know what that shining is, mates? Why, it's the glow of timbers that's been rotted by near two hundred years of weather."

"Softly, Tom!" said another; "'tis Hell that owns her crew; they have the malice of devils, and they need but touch us to founder us."

"Wait, and you shall see her melt!" exclaimed one of the two foreigners who were among our company of seamen. "If she is, as I believe, she will be manned by the ghosts of wicked men who have perished at sea; presently a bell shall strike, and she must disappear!"

As this was said there was a commotion forward, and the carpenter, borne by two stout hands, was carried into the midst of the crew, and propped up so that he might see the ship. I was as eager as any of the most illiterate sailors on board to hear what he had to say, and took a step the better to catch his words. A whole minute went by whilst he gazed; so strained and anticipative were my senses that the moments seemed as hours. He then said, "Mates, yonder's the Death

Ship, right enough. Look hard, and you'll mark the steeve of her bowsprit with the round top at the end of it, and the spring of her aft in a fashion more ancient than is the ages of any two of the oldest men aboard. Note the after-rake of her mizzen-mast, and how the heel of the fore-mast looks to step in the fore-peak. That's the ship—born in 1650 —Vanderdecken master—what I've often heard tell of—raise my head, mates!"

And here, whether through pain or weakness or horror, he fainted, but being laid upon the deck, and some water thrown over his face, he came to in a short while, and lay trembling, refusing to speak or answer questions.

A slight thinning of the vapour that hid the moon had enabled us to remark those points in the ship the carpenter had named; and whilst he was being recovered from his swoon, the moon looked down from a gulf in the mist, but her light was still very tarnished

and dim, though blurred and distorted as was
her appearance, yet there instantly formed
round her the same halo or wan circle that
was visible before she was hidden. But her
apparition made a light that exquisitely
answered to those two lines of Shakespeare—

" Therefore the moon, the governess of floods,
    Pale in her anger washes all the air."

For such radiance as fell really seemed like a
cleansing of the atmosphere after the black
smother that had encompassed us, and now
we could all see the ship distinctly as she lay
on our quarter with her broadside somewhat
to us, her yards trimmed like our own, and
her sails hanging dead.

It was the solemnest sight that ever morta.
eye beheld. The light left her black, so
there was no telling what hue she showed or
was painted. Her bows lay low in the water
after the old fashion, with head-boards curling
to her beak, that doubtless bore an ornament,
though we could not distinguish it. There

she rose like a hill, broken with the bulwarks
that defined her waist, quarter-deck and short
poop. This was as much as we could
discern of her hull. Her foremast stood
close to where the heel of her bowsprit came;
her mizzen-mast raked over her stern, and
upon it was a yard answering to the rig of a
felucca; the clew of its sail came down clear
of a huge lantern whose iron frame, for all
the glass in it was broke and gone, showed
like the skeleton of some monster on her
taffrail. It was a sight to terrify the stoutest
heart to see the creeping of thin, worm or
wire-like gleamings upon the side she showed
to us. I considered at first she was glossy
and that those lights were the reflection of
the phosphoric fires in the water under her;
but it was soon made plain that this was not
so, as, though to be sure a greenish glare of
the true sea-flame would show against or near
her when she slightly leaned, as we did, to
the swell, this charnel-house or touch-wood

glimmer played all along her without regard to the phosphorescence under her.

Now, ever since I was first going to sea, I had, as I have said, believed in the existence of the Spectre Ship, which all mariners I have sailed with feared to encounter; but so many imaginative stories had come of her—some feigning, as the carpenter's version showed, that she was a death ship, filled with spectres who navigated her; others that she was a spectral bark, laden with souls, against whom the gates of Purgatory were closed; others that she was a vessel for ever beating against gales of wind, sometimes appearing in a tempest that surrounded her when the rest of the ocean was smooth, sometimes rising from the waves, sometimes floating among the clouds, buffetting up there as though the masses of insubstantial vapour were solid and massy folds and acclivities; I say I had heard so many stories that they had ended in leaving

me with a belief of my own, which was that
the Phantom Ship—rightly so named—was
an airy incorporeal thing—a vision to be
encountered but rarely in these parts, a sea-
ghost that had been too often beheld in the
course of years to be denied, and as truly a
spectre in its way as any that may be read of
in Holy Writ, or that has stood at the bed-
sides of men and women and delivered
messages from futurity.

This being my belief, then, though I was
mightily terrified by the ancient shape of the
ship and the mystery of her purpose, and the
darkness and silence that clothed her, I could
not believe that she was the true spectre that
the sailor dreads ; for, that she was as substantial as our vessel—"a quarry of stout
spurs and knotted fangs "—was undeniable,
not more from her quiet, heaving motion
than from the dull sounds I had now and
again caught of the movement of her gear
aloft, such as the scraping of a rope in a

block, or the soft slap of a cloth against a spar by the heave of the fabric setting some light sail a-fanning.

"What think you of her, Fenton?" said Mr. Hall, speaking softly, but with much of his excitement and uneasiness gone. "Does she resemble the craft that the master of the snow told Captain Skevington he sighted hereabouts?"

"Why, yes, I think so," said I; "but it does not follow that she is the Phantom Ship. The Plymouth hooker's yarn owed a good deal to terror, and it would not lose in its passage through the brain of a lunatic, as I fear poor Skevington was."

"She has a very solid look—she is a real ship, but the like of her I have never seen, save in old prints. Mark those faint fiery stripes and spirals upon her. I do not understand it. The wood that yields such light must be as rotten as tinder and porous as a sponge. It could not swim."

By this time the mysterious ship had
floated out her whole length, unless it were
our vessel that had slewed and given us that
view of her.   No light save the lambent
gleams on her sides was to be seen.   We
could hear no voices.   We could discern no
movement of figures or distinguish any out-
line resembling a human shape upon her.
On a sudden, my eye was caught by an
illumination overhead that made a lustre
strong enough to enable me to see the face
of Mr. Hall.   I looked up conceiving that
one of our crew had jumped aloft with a
lantern, and saw at our main yard-arm a
corpus sant or St. Elmo's light, that shone
freely like a luminous bulb, poised a few
inches above the spar.   Scarce had this been
kindled, and whilst it was paling the faces of
our seamen who stared at it, there suddenly
shone two bright meteors of a similar kind
upon the strange ship ; one on top of the
topgallant-masthead that was the full height

of the main spars, and one on the summit of a
mast that stood up from the round top at the
end of the bowsprit and that in olden times,
before it was discontinued, would have
been called the sprit-topmast.   They had
something of the glory of stars ; their reflection twisted like silver serpents in the dark
waters ; and as though they had been flam-
beaux or lamps, they flung their spectral
glow upon the strangely-cut sails of the
vessel, upon her rigging and spars, sickling
all things to their starry colour, dimly illumin-
ating even the distant castle-like poop, showing clearly the dark line of bulwarks, whilst a
deeper dye of blackness entered into the hull
from the shadow between the *corpus sants* on
high and their mirroring beneath.

"Thanks be to God for the sight of those
lights!" exclaimed a deep voice, sounding out
among the men.   "It's a saint's hand as
kindles them, I've heared ; and there'll be a
breeze with luck behind it presently,"

"See, Mr. Hall!" cried I, pointing; "do you observe the figures of men? Look along the line of the forecastle—one, two, three—I count six there; and look right aft on that bit of a poop. Do you mark a couple of shapes viewing us as if with folded arms?"

"Yes!" He paused, staring, then added, "Those lights are familiar enough to me, I've seen them scores of times," speaking in whispers, which trembled back to their former notes of consternation, "but there's something frightful about them now—and yonder one," pointing to our yard-arm, "and the sight they show. She's no natural ship," he said, pulling off his cap, and passing his hand over his forehead. "Would to God a breeze would come and part us."

"Hail him again, sir!"

"Hail him you, my throat is dry."

I walked right aft to bring me more abreast of the silent motionless figures on the stranger's poop, and jumping on to the rail caught hold of the vang of the spanker-gaff to steady myself, and putting a hand to my mouth, roared out, "Ship ahoy! What ship is that?" and stopped breathless, so that I seemed to hear the echoes of my own voice among the sails of the stranger.

"What ship is that?" now came back in a deep, organ-like note, and the two figures separated, one walking forward, and the other stepping, as I had, on to the bulwark over the quarter-gallery.

"The Saracen, of London, bound to Indian ports," I responded.

"I will send a boat!" cried the man, in the same deep-throated voice.

"If you do, we'll fire into it!" screamed a seaman on our deck. "Mates—Mr. Hall, you see now what he is! Keep them off!— keep them off!" at which there was a sudden hurrying of feet, with many clicking sounds of triggers sharply cocked, by which I knew our men had armed themselves.

The *corpus sant* at our yard-arm vanished;
in a few seconds it showed itself afresh mid-
way up the mainmast, making a wild light
all around it; those on the stranger burned
steadily, and I believed a third had been
kindled on her till I saw it was a lantern
carried along the deck. There was a stillness lasting some minutes. What they were
about we could not see; anon came a creaking, as of ropes travelling in blocks, then a
light splash; the lantern dropped jerkily
down the ship's side, plainly grasped by a
man; flashes of phosphorus broke out of the
water to the dip of oars, like fire clipped from
a flint. I felt a faint air blowing, but did not
heed it, being half-frenzied with the excitement and fear raised in me by what I could
now see—thanks to the light of the St. Elmo
fires, and the mystic crawlings of flames on
the vessel's sides. I saw a boat, square at
both ends, with the gunwale running out into
horns, rowed by two figures, whilst a third

stood upright in the bows, holding high a lighted lantern in one hand, and extending his other arm in a posture of supplication.

At this instant a yellow glare broke in a noon-tide dazzle from our own ship's rail, and the thunder of twenty muskets fired at once fell upon my hearing. I started with the violence of the shock breaking in upon me, heedlessly let go the vang that I had been grasping with my left hand, and fell headlong overboard.

CHAPTER XII.

I ROSE to the surface from a deep plunge, but being a very indifferent swimmer it was as much as I could do—clothed as I was—to keep myself afloat by battling with my hands. I heard the rippling of the water about my ears, and I felt a deep despair settle upon my spirits, for I knew that the air that blew would carry my ship away from me and that I must speedily drown.

Indeed, to the first impulse of wind the Saracen had moved and I could see her, a great shadow, drawing away with the *corpus sant*, that a minute before had sparkled on her mainmast, now shining on her fore-topsail yard-arm. I had not the least doubt

that, in the noise of the shooting, and amid
the general alarm excited by the approach of
the boat, neither the splash I had made in
striking the water nor my disappearance had
been noticed, and I remember thinking with
the swiftness peculiar to persons in my
situation—for as Cowper says—

> " He long survives who lives an hour
> In ocean self-upheld——"

I say I remember thinking that even if I
should be immediately missed it was most
unlikely the crew would suffer Mr. Hall to
stop the ship and seek for me, for they would
be mad not to use the new wind and sweep
away from waters accurst by the presence of
what was undoubtedly the Death Ship,
whilst if even Mr. Hall's persuasion should
prevail, yet long before that time I should
have sunk.

I struggled hard to keep myself afloat,
freely breaking the water in the hope that the
light and whiteness of it might be seen.

Four or five minutes thus passed and I was feeling my legs growing weighty as lead, when I noticed a light approach me. My eyes being full of wet, I could see no more than the light, what held or bore it being eclipsed by the spikes or fibres that shot out of it; as you notice a candle flame when the sight is damp. I could also hear the dip and trickle of oars, and tried to shout; but my brain was giddy, my mind sinking into a babbling state, and in truth I was so exhausted, that but for the sudden life darted into me by the sight of the lamp, I am sure I should then and there have clenched my hands above my head and sunk.

The lantern was flashed full upon my face and I was grasped by my hair. He who seized me spoke, and I believed it was the voice of one of the men in my watch, though I did not catch a syllable of his speech. After which I felt myself grasped under each arm and lifted out of the water, whereupon I no doubt fainted, for there is a blank between this and what followed, though the interval must have been very short.

When I opened my eyes, or rather when my senses returned to me, I found myself lying on my back, and the first thing I noticed was the moon shining weakly amid thin bodies of vapour which the wind had set in motion and which sped under her in puffs like the smoke of gunpowder after the discharge of a cannon. I lay musing a little while, conscious of nothing but the moon and some dark stretches of sail hovering above me; but my mind gathering force, I saw by the cut of the canvas that I was on board a strange ship; and then did I observe three men standing near my feet watching me. A great terror seized my heart. I sprang erect with a loud cry of fear, and rushed to the rail to see if the Saracen was near that I might hail her, but was stayed in that by being seized by the arm.

He who clutched me exclaimed in Dutch, "What would you do? If you could swim for a week you would not catch her."

I perfectly understood him, but made no reply, did not even look at him, staring about the sea for the Saracen in an anguish of mind not to be expressed. Suddenly I caught sight of the smudge of her, and perceived she was heading away on her course; she was out on our starboard beam. I cast my eyes aloft, and found the yards of the ship I was in braced up to meet the wind on the larboard tack, whence I knew that every instant was widening the space between the two vessels. On mastering this I could have dashed myself down on the deck with grief and terror. One of the group observing me as if I should fall, extended his hand, but I shrunk back with horror, and covered my face, whilst deep hysteric sobs burst from my breast, for now, without heeding any further appearances, I knew that I was on board the

Phantom Ship, the Sea Spectre, dreaded of marines, a fabric accurst by God, in the presence of men dead and yet alive, more terrible in their supernatural existence, in their clothing of flesh whose human mortality had been rendered undecaying by a fate that shrunk up the soul in one to think of, than had they been ghosts—essences through which you might pass your hand as through a moonbeam !

I stood awhile as though paralysed, but was presently rallied by the chill of the night wind striking through my streaming clothes. A lantern was near where the three men were grouped, no doubt the same that had been carried in the boat, but the dim illumination would have sufficed for no more than to throw out the proportion of things within its sphere, had it not been helped by the faint moonlight and a *corpus sant* that shone with the power of a planet close against the blocks of the jeers of the mainyard. 'Twas a ghostly radiance to behold the men in, but I found nerve now to survey them.

There were three, as I have said : one very tall, above six feet, with a grey—almost white—beard, that descended to his waist ; the second was a broad, corpulent man, of the true Dutch build without hair on his face ; in the third man I could see nothing striking, if it were not for a ruggedness of seafaring aspect. I could not distinguish their apparel beyond that the stout man wore boots to the height of his knees, whereas the tall personage was clad in black hose, shoes with large buckles, and breeches terminating at the knees ; their head-dresses were alike, a sort of cap of skin, with flaps for the ears.

" Do you speak Dutch ?" said the tallest of the three, after eyeing me in silence whilst a man could have counted a hundred. He it was who had responded to my hail from the Saracen, as my ear immediately detected— now that I had my faculties—by the deep,

organ-like melodiousness and tremor of his
voice.

I answered "Yes."

"Why were your people afraid of us?
We intended no harm. We desired but a
little favour—a small quantity of tobacco,
of which we are short."

This speech I followed, though some of
the words, or the pronunciation of them,
were different from what I had been used
to hear at Rotterdam. He spoke impe-
-riously, with a hint even of passion, and,
rearing himself to his full stature, clasped
his hands behind him, and stared at me as
some Indian King might at a slave.

"Sir," said I, speaking brokenly, for I was
a slow hand at his tongue, and besides, the
chill of my clothes was now become a pain,
"first let me ask what ship is this, and who
are you and your men who have rescued me
from death?"

"The name of this ship is the Braave,

he answered, in his deep, solemn voice.
"I, who command the vessel, am known
as Cornelius Vanderdecken; the three seamen, to whom you owe your life, are
Frederick Houtman, John de Bremen, and
this man," indicating the rough, uncouth
person who stood on his left, "the mate,
Herman Van Vogelaar."

I felt a sensation as of ice pressed to my
chest when he pronounced his own name,
yet, recollecting he had called his ship the
Braave, I asked, though 'twas wonderful he
could follow my utterance—

"What port do you belong to?"

"Amsterdam."

"Where are you from?"

"Batavia."

I said, "When did you sail?"

"On the twenty-second of July in last
year! By the glory of the Holy Trinity, but
it is dreary work; see how the wind heads us
even yet!" He sighed deeply and glanced

aloft in a manner that suggested grievous weariness.

"Last year!" I thought, a sudden elation expanding my soul and calming me as an opiate might, "if that be so why, then, though this ship had made a prodigiously long voyage of it from Java to these parallels, there is nothing wildly out of nature in such tardiness." Last year! Had I caught the true signification of the words he used?

"Pray, sir," said I, speaking in as firm a voice as the shivers which chased me permitted, "what might last year be?"

The mate, Van Vogelaar, growled out some exclamation I could not catch, the captain made a gesture with his hands, whilst their burly companion said in thick, Dutch accents, "It needs not salt water, but good, strong liquor to take away a Hollander's brain."

"Last year!" exclaimed Vanderdecken, un-

bending his haughty, imperious manner,
" why, mynheer, what should be last year but
1653 ?"

CHAPTER XIII.

WY ZYN AL VERDOMD.

WHEN he said this I felt like one in whom there is suddenly wrought a dual action of the brain; where from one side, so to say, there is darted into the mind thoughts utterly illogical and insane, which the same side marvels at, and seeks to reject, though if the fit linger the whole intelligence may be seized.

I recollect of seeking for confirmation of the words of the man who styled himself Vanderdecken, in the ship, and of noticing, for the first time, that upon the planks of the deck which were out of the reach of the *corpus sant*, were the same crawling, elusive fires, as of phosphorus, creeping and coming

and going upon a dark wall, which I had
observed on the vessel's sides. Several
figures of men moved forward. Close
beside me was a small gun of the kind
carried by ships in the beginning of the
last century, termed a light saker, and discharging a six-pound ball. There were
three of these on the larboard side, and, in
the haze of the moonlight and the sheen of
the jelly-like star that shone with a pure,
pale gold over my head, I could discern
upon the bulwarks of the quarter-deck and
poop several swivels furnished with handles
for pointing them. I also observed a short
flight of steps conducting to the quarter-deck,
with two sets of a like kind leading to the
poop, the front of which was furnished with
a door and little window.

These matters I took in with a sweep of
the eye, for the light was confusing, a faint,
erroneous ray glancing from imperfect surfaces and flinging half an image; and then

an indescribable fear possessing me again, I looked in the direction where I had last beheld the smudge made by the Saracen, and, not seeing her, cried out wildly, in my broken Dutch, "Sirs, for the love of God follow my ship, and make some signals that she may know I am here!"

"Skipper," exclaimed the smooth-faced, corpulent man, who proved to be the boatswain, named Antony Jans, "after their cowardly inhumanity in firing upon a small unarmed boat, and putting in peril the life of our mate, Van Vogelaar, we should have nothing more to do with her."

"Henceforth this Englishman will know that the Dutch are a merciful people," said Van Vogelaar, scornfully. "Had our nationalities been reversed, he would have been left to drown as a tribute to the courage of his comrades."

Whilst this was said, Vanderdecken continued to regard me steadfastly and with great sternness, then on a sudden relaxing his frown, he exclaimed in that wondrous voice of his, which put a solemn music into his least utterance: "Come, you shiver with the cold, and have the look of the drowned. Jans, send Prins to me; sir, please to follow."

He motioned in a haughty manner towards the poop and walked that way. One desperate look I cast round the sea, and then with a prayer to God that this experience might prove some eclipse of my reason from which my mind would float out bright afresh ere long, I followed the great figure of the captain, but with a step so faltering from weakness and grief, that he, perceiving my condition, took me by the elbow and supported me up the ladder to the cabin under the poop.

Whether it was this courtesy or owing to a return of my manhood — and I trust the reader will approve the candour with which I have confessed my cowardice — whatever

might be the reason, I began now to look
about me with a growing curiosity. The interior into which Captain Vanderdecken conducted me, was of a dingy yellowish hue,
such as age might complexion delicate white
paint with. An oil lamp of a very beautiful,
elegant and rare pattern, furnished with eight
panes of glass, variously and all choicely
coloured with figures of birds, flowers and
the like, though the opening at the bottom
let the white light of the oil-flame fall fair on
to the table and the deck, swung by a thin
chain from a central beam. The cabin was
the width of the ship, and on its walls were
oval frames, dusky as old mahogany, each
one, as I suspected, holding a painting. Over
the door by which the cabin was entered was
a clock and near it hung a cage with a parrot
in it. Of ports I could see no remains, and
supposed that by day all the light that
entered streamed through the windows on
either side the door.

The deck was dark as with age. At the
after end there were two state cabins bulk-
headed off from the living room, each with
a door. The several colours of the lamp
caused it to cast a radiance like a rainbow,
and therefore it was hard to make sure of
objects amid such an intricacy of illumination;
but, as I have said, the sides of the cabin were
a sickly dismal yellow, and the furniture in it
was formed of a very solid square table, with
legs marvellously carved, and a box beneath
it, two benches on either hand, and a black
high-backed chair — the back of withered
velvet, the wood framing it cut into many
devices—at the head or sternmost end of it.

All these things were matters to be quickly
noticed. The captain, first removing his cap,
pointed to a bench, and lifting his finger, with
a glance at the starboard cabin, said in a low
tone, "Sir, if you speak be it softly, if you
please," and then directed his eyes towards
the entrance from the deck, standing erect,

with one hand on the table, and manifestly waiting for the person he had styled Prins to arrive. A ruby-coloured lustre was upon his face; his waist down was in the white lamplight. He had a most noble port, I thought, such an elevation of the head, such disdainful and determined erectness of figure, as made his posture royal. There was not the least hint in his face of the Dutch flatness and insipidity of expression one is used to in those industrious but phlegmatic people. His nose was aquiline, the nostrils hidden by the moustachios which mingled with his noble Druidical beard. His forehead was square and heavy, his hair was scanty, yet abundant enough to conceal the skin of his head; his eyes were black, impassioned, relentless, and a ruby star now shone in each which gave them a forbidding and formidable expression as they moved under the shadow of his shaggy brows. He wore a coat of stout cloth confined by buttons, and a belt round his waist. This, with his small clothes which I have described, formed a very puzzling apparel, the like of which I had never seen. There were no rents, nor darns nor patches —nothing to indicate that his attire was of great age. Yet there was something in this commanding person that caused me to know, by feelings deeper than awe or even fear, by instincts indeed not explicable, such as must have urged in olden times the intelligence to the recognition of those supernatural beings you read of in Scripture, that he was not as I was, as are other men who bear their natural parts in the procession from the cradle to the grave. The tremendous and shocking fears of Captain Skevington recurred to me, and methought as I gazed at the silent, majestic seaman, that the late master of the Saracen who, by his ending, had shown himself a madman might, as had other insane persons in their time, have struck in one of his finer frenzies upon a horrible truth ; the mere fear of which caused me to press my hands to my eyes with a renewal of mental anguish, and to entreat in a swift prayer to that Being, whom he who stood before me had defied, for power to collect my mind and for quick deliverance from this awful situation.

Not a syllable fell from the captain till the arrival of Prins, a parched-faced, bearded man, habited in a coarse woollen shirt, trousers of the stuff we call fearnought, and an old jacket. He made nothing of my presence nor condition, scarce glancing at me.

"Get this Englishman a change of clothes," said the captain. "Take what may be needful from my cabin. They will hang loose on him but must serve till his own are dry. Quick! you see he shivers."

All this was expressed in Dutch, but as I have before said, of an antique character, and therefore not quickly to be followed;

whence I will not pretend that I give exactly all that was spoken, though the substance of it is accurately reported.

The man styled Prins went to the larboard cabin at the end, whilst the captain, going to the table, pulled from under it a great drawer, which I had taken to be a chest, from which he lifted a silver goblet and a strangely-fashioned stone bottle.

"Drink, sir," he exclaimed, with a certain arrogant impetuosity in his way of pouring out the liquor and extending the goblet.

'Twas neat brandy, and the dose a large mouthful; I tossed down the whole of it, and placed the goblet, that was very heavy and sweetly chased, on the table with a bow of thanks.

"That will put fire into your blood," said he, returning the cup and bottle to the drawer, and then folding his arms and looking at me under his contracted brows, with his back to the lantern whilst he leaned against the table. "Are you fresh from your country?"

I told him that we had sailed in April from the Thames, and had lately come out of Table Bay.

"Is there peace between your nation and mine?" he inquired, speaking softly, as though he feared to awaken some sleeper, though, let his utterance be what it would, 'twas always melodious and rich.

I answered, "No; it grieves me to say it, but our countries are still at war. I will not pretend, sir, that Great Britain has acted with good faith towards the Batavian Republic; their High Mightinesses resent the infraction of treaties; they protest against the manner in which the island of St. Eustatia was devastated; they hope to recover the Cape of Good Hope, and likewise their possessions in the Indies, more particularly their great Coromandel factory."

Mere courtesy would have taught me

to speak as soothingly as possible of such things. though, but for the brandy, I doubt if my teeth would not have chattered too boisterously for the utterance of even the few words I delivered. In honest truth, I felt an unspeakable awe and fear in addressing this man, who surveyed me with the severest, most scornful gaze imaginable from the height of his regal stature.

"Of what are you speaking?" he exclaimed, after a frowning stare of amazement; then waved his hand with a gesture half of pity, half of disdain. "You have been perilously close to death," he continued, "and this idle babble will settle into good sense when you have shifted and slept." He smiled contemptuously with a half-look around, as though he sought another of his own kind to address, and said as one thinking aloud, "If Tromp and Evertzens and De Witt and De Ruyter have not yet swept them off the seas 'tis only because they have not had time to complete the easy task !"

As he said this the clock over the door struck two. The chimes had a hollow, cathedral-like sound, as though indeed it was the clock of a cathedral striking in the distance. Glancing at the direction whence these notes issued, I was just in time to witness the acting of an extraordinary piece of mechanism, that is to say, there arose to the top of the clock-case, that was of some species of metal—the dial plate of blue enamel protected with horn instead of glass—there arose, I say, the figure of a skeleton, imitated to the life, holding in one hand an hour-glass on which he turned his eyeless sockets by a movement of the head, whilst with the other hand he grasped a lance or spear that, as I afterwards perceived, he flourished to every stroke of the clock-bell, as though he pierced something prostrate at his feet. The figure shrank into the inside of the clock when the

chimes were over. As if to complete the
bewilderment under which I laboured, scarce
had the second chime of the clock rung its
last vibration, when a harsh voice croaked
out in Dutch—

"Wy Zyn al Verdomd!"

I started, and cried out involuntarily and
faintly, "My God!"

"It was the parrot that spoke," said
Captain Vanderdecken, with a softening of
his looks, though he did not smile. "'Tis the
only sentence she seems able to pronounce.
It was all she could say when I bought her."

"Have you had her long, sir?" I inquired,
feeling as though I lay a-dreaming.

"I bought her from a Chinaman of
Batavia two days before we sailed as a gift
for my eldest daughter——"

Here he was interrupted by the arrival of
Prins. "The clothes are ready, skipper,"
said he.

On this Vanderdecken, motioning me to

be silent—a piece of behaviour that was as puzzling as all other things—conducted me to the cabin from which Prins had emerged, and viewing the clothes upon the bed, said, "Yes, they will do ; wear them, mynheer, till yours have been dried. Leave this door on the hook, you will then get light enough for your purpose from yonder lamp."

The dress consisted of warm knitted stockings, breeches of an old pattern, and a coat with a great skirt embellished with metal buttons, several of which were missing, and the remains of some gold lace upon the cuffs. In addition, there was a clean linen shirt, and a pair of South American hide boots, fawn-coloured. 'Twas like clothing myself for a masquerade to dress in such things, but for all that I was mighty pleased and grateful to escape from my own soaked attire, which by keeping the surface of the body cold prohibited my nerves from regaining their customary tone. I went to work nimbly, observing that Captain Vanderdecken waited for me, and was soon shifted, but not before I had viewed the cabin, which I found to be spacious enough. The bed was curious, being what we term a four-poster, the upper ends of the posts cleated to the ceiling, whilst the lower legs were in the form of dolphins, and had one time been gilt with gold. There were curtains to it of faded green silk —as I judged—ragged in places. There were lockers, a small table, on which lay a forestaff, or cross-staff as it was often called, a rude ancient instrument used for measuring the altitude of the sun before the introduction of Hadley's quadrant, and formed of a wooden staff, having a scale of degrees and parts of degrees marked upon it, and cross-pieces which could be moved along it. By it stood a sand-glass for turning to tell the time by. Against the bulkhead that separated this from the adjoining cabin were hung two ox-

eyed mirrors, the frames whereof had been
gilt, also four small paintings in oak-coloured
borders richly beaded. I could see that they
were portraits of females, dim, the hues
being faded. The ceiling of this cabin
showed traces of having been, once on
a time, very handsomely painted with the
hand.

Other things I noticed were a copper
speaking-trumpet and an ancient perspective
glass—such as poets of Vanderdecken's time
would style an optic tube — very weighty,
and formed of two tubes. This thing stood
on brackets, under which hung a watch, of as
true a sphere as an orange, and of the size of
one.

Indeed, look where you would, you could
not fail to guess how stout and noble a
ship this Braave, as her captain named her,
must have been in those distant years which
witnessed her birth.

My costume made me feel ridiculous

enough, for, whereas the boots might have
belonged to a period when Shelvocke and
Clipperton were plundering the Spaniards in
the south seas, the coat was of a fashion of
about thirty years past, whilst the breeches
were such as merchant captains and mates
wore when I was first going to sea. However, being changed and dry, I stepped forth,
bearing my wet clothes with me, but they
were immediately taken from me by Prins,
who had been standing near the door unperceived by me. On my appearing, Captain
Vanderdecken rose from the chair at the
head of the table, but seemed to find
nothing in my dress to amuse him. The
vari-coloured light was extremely confusing,
and it was with the utmost pains that I
could discern the expression of his face, but,
so far as I made out, it was one of extreme
melancholy, touched with lights and shades
by his moods, which yet left the prevailing
character unchanged. Indeed, the dreadful

fancies of Captain Skevington smote me fiercely once again, for, as I live to say it, the countenance of this tall and haughty sea-man did suggest to me the melancholy you notice on the face of the dead—meaningless as that look in them may be—but in his case irradiated by the tints and expressions of vitality, insomuch that I fully felt the force of the remark the master of the Plymouth snow had made to Captain Skevington touch-ing the man he had seen on board the Death Ship, namely, that he was a corpse artificially animated and most terrible to behold for his suggestions of death-in-life.

" Will you go to rest ?" said he.

" I am willing to do whatever you desire," said I. " Your kindness is great and I thank you for it."

"Ay," he replied, "spite of the war I'd liefer serve an Englishman than one of any other country. The old and the young Commonwealths should be friends. On

either hand there are mighty hearts, you in
your Blakes, your Ayscues, your Monks;
we in our Van Tromp, whom the King of
Denmark, to my great joy before I sailed,
honourably justified to the people of Holland,
and in Van Galen, Ruyter, with other skilled
and lion-hearted men, whom I shall glory in
greeting on my return."

He seemed to reflect a moment, and suddenly cried, with a passionate sparkle in his
eyes, " But 'twas cowardly in your captain to
order his men to fire upon our boat.   What
did we seek?   Such tobacco as you could
have spared, which we were willing to purchase.   By the vengeance of Heaven, 'twas a
deed unworthy of Englishmen."

I did not dare explain the true cause, and
said, gently, " Sir, our captain lay dead in his
cabin. The men, missing the chief, fell into a
panic at the sight of this ship, for she showed
large in the dusk, and we feared you meant
to lay us aboard."

" Enough !" he exclaimed, imperiously.
" Follow me to your cabin."

He led the way on to the deck and we
descended the quarter-deck ladder.

CHAPTER XIV.

I HAD been in too great a confusion of mind
to heed the movements of the ship whilst I
was under cover, but on emerging I now
noticed that it had come on to blow very
fresh. The vessel under larboard tacks—I
could not see what canvas she carried—lay
along very much, being light and tall, and
rolled with peculiar clumsiness in the hollows.
I caught sight of the water over the weather-
rail, and judged with the eye of a seaman
that what progress she was making was
wholly leeway ; so that we were being blown
dead to the eastward, without probably
"reaching," as it is termed, by so much as
half-a-knot an hour. The moon was now

deep in the west and showing a very wan and stormy disk.   North-west, where the land lay, the sea looked to rise into a fluid blackness of thunder-clouds, wherefrom even as I glanced that way there fell a red gash of lightning.   There was a heavy sound of seething and bombarding billows all about us, and the whole picture had a wildness past language, what with the scarlet glare of the northern levin-brands and the ghastly tempestuous paleness of the westering moon and a dingy faintness owing its existence to I know not what, if it were not the light of the foaming multitudinous surge reflected upon the sooty bosoms of the lowering clouds over our stern.

Captain Vanderdecken stood for a moment looking round upon this warring scene, and flung up his arms towards the moon with a passionate savage gesture, and then strode to a narrow hatch betwixt the limits of the quarter-deck and the mainmast, down

which he went, first turning to see if I
followed. I now found myself in a kind
of 'tween-decks, with two cabins on either
hand, in the doorway of the fore one, on
the starboard side, stood the man Prins,
holding a small lantern.

" This, sir," said Vanderdecken, pointing
to the cabin, "must serve you for a sleeping
room ; it has not the comfort of an inn, but
'tis easy to see you are a sailor, and, therefore, one to whom a plank will often be a
soft couch. In any case, here is accommo-
dation warmer than the bottom of the ocean."

With a cold and condescending salute he
withdrew. Prins hung the lantern on to a
rail beside the door, and said he would return
for it shortly. I wanted to ask the man some
questions about the ship and her commander,
but there was something about him so scaring
and odd that I could not summon up heart to
address him. He appeared as one in whom
all qualities of the soul are dead, acting, in

sooth, like a sleep-walker, giving me not the least heed whatever, and going about his business as mechanically as the skeleton in the cabin clock rose and darted his lance to the chimes of the bell.

The compartment in which I was to sleep was empty of all furniture saving a locker that served as a seat as well as a box, and a wooden sleeping-place, formed of planks, secured to the side, in which, in lieu of a mattress, were a couple of stout blankets, tolerably new, and a sailor's bag, filled with straw, for a pillow. I was wearied to the bone, yet not sleepy, and lay me down in my strange clothes without so much as removing my boots, and in a few minutes Prins arrived and took away the light, and there I was in pitch darkness.

And yet I should not say this, for, though to be sure no sensible reflection penetrated the blackness, yet when the lamp was removed and my eyes had lost the glare of it, I

beheld certain faint crawlings and swarmings
of phosphoric light upon the beams and
bulkheads, such as were noticeable upon the
outside of the ship, only not so strong. I
likewise observed a cold and ancient smell,
such as I recollect once catching the breath
of in the hold of a ship that had been built in
1702 and which people in the year 1791 or
thereabouts viewed as a curiosity. Otherwise
there was nothing else remarkable. Whatever this vessel might be, her motion on the
seas was as natural as that of the Saracen,
only that her wallowing was more ponderous
and ungainly. Yet, merciful Heaven! how
did every bulkhead groan, how did every
timber complain, how did every treenail cry
aloud! The noise of the labouring was truly
appalling ; the creaking, straining, jarring, as
though the whole fabric were being dashed
to pieces. I had not immediately noticed
this when I followed Captain Vanderdecken
below, but it grew upon my ears as I lay in

the blackness. Yet they were natural sounds,
and as such they afforded a sort of relief to
my strained brain and nervous, yea, and
affrighted imagination. The stillness of a
dead calm would have maddened me, I truly
believe. Phantasms and other horrors of my
fancy, rendered delirious by the situation into
which I had been plunged, would have played
their parts upon that stage of blackness,
hideous with the vault-like stirring of the
glow of rotted timber, to the destruction of
my intellect, but for the homely thunder of
the sea without and the crazy echoes within.

I asked myself what ship was this? That
she had a supernatural life, that he who
styled himself Vanderdecken—which tradition
reported was the name of the master of the
Phantom Ship, though it has been averred
that his real name was Bernard Fokke—I
say that he and the others I had seen, more
particularly the man Prins, had something
goblin-like about them, something that carried

them far out of the range of our common
humanity, spite of the majestic port, the
noble presence, the thrilling tones, like the
music of distant summer thunder, of the commander, I could no more question than the
beating of my own heart as I lay a-thinking.
I knew by what I had heard and viewed
already, even in the brief hours packed full of
consternation, during which I had been on
her, that I was aboard of the Flying Dutchman, the Phantom Ship, the Death Ship, the
Sea Spectre, as she has variously been
termed.

Yet there was so much to puzzle me that I
was fit to lapse into idiotcy. If Vanderdecken
had sailed from Batavia in 1653, why did he
speak of it as last year? If the Death Ship
was a ghostly object, impalpable, an essence
only as is a spirit, why was this vessel so
substantial that, heavily as she resounded
with the crazy echoes of her material state,
no first-rate could hold a stouter conflict with

the seas? If she had been battling off the Agulhas for one hundred and forty-three years, how came she to have oil and waste for her lanterns, clothes such as I wore, such as the men I had seen were habited in, brandy, blankets almost new like those I lay on, and other stores; for I might be sure, from the jar of brandy the captain had produced, that the crew ate and drank as all men do and must!

These and other points I could not reconcile to my conviction that the ship I was aboard of was the craft dreaded by all men because of the great God's ban upon her and the misfortunes she brought to others with the very winds which filled her canvas. I would have given all I owned—though, alack! that would have been small enough if I lost what belonged to me in the Saracen—for leave to keep the deck, but I did not venture for fear of incurring the displeasure of Vanderdecken. So for several hours did I lay

broad awake in my black dungeon of a cabin,
watching the loathsome, ghostly phosphoric
glow all about me, and listening to the
bellowing of the wind that had grown into
a storm, and marking the furious rolling of
the ship, whose wild inner creakings put a
note of frenzy into the thunder of the gale ;
but never once hearing the sound of a
human call nor the echo of a man's tread,
I then fell asleep, but not before the dawn
had broken, as I might tell by the radiance,
which was little better than an ashen twilight,
that streamed down the hatch and showed in
an open space above the cabin door.

CHAPTER XV.

I INSPECT THE FLYING DUTCHMAN.

I HAD scarcely fully woke up, when the man
Prins opened the cabin door and peered in,
and perceiving me to be awake, he entered
bearing a metal pitcher of water, an earthen-
ware dish, and a rough cloth for drying the
skin. He put down the dish so that it could
not slide, for the ship was rolling very heavily,
and then poured water into it, and said, as
he was in the act of withdrawing with the
pitcher, "The skipper is on the poop."

I answered by asking him for my clothes.
He shook his bearded, parchment-coloured
face and said: "They are still sodden," and
immediately went out.

I might have guessed they could not be

dry, but I presented so hideous a figure in
the apparel that had been lent to me that
I should have been glad to resume my own
coat and breeches, wet or no wet; but there
was no help for it. I rose and plunged my
face in the cold water, used my fingers for a
comb, which sufficed, since I commonly wore
my hair rough, having much of it and hating
a tye, and putting on my hat that had held to
my head in the water, and that had not been
taken from me to dry, I stepped out of the
cabin, climbed the steps that led through the
hatch, and gained what was in former times
termed the upper deck; for let me make you
understand me by explaining that, beginning
right aft, first there was a poop-deck eleva-
ted above the quarter-deck, which in its turn
was raised above the upper-deck, along which
you walked till you arrived at the forecastle
that went flush or level to the bows and was
fortified by tall, stout bulwarks, with ports for
fore-chasers.

For some considerable while I stood near
the hatch gazing about me, as this was my
first view of the ship by daylight. Right
opposite soared the mainmast, an immensely
thick "made" spar, weightier than we should
now think of using for a craft twice this
vessel's size; the top was a large circular
platform, protected by a fence-work half as
tall as a man, looped for the projection of
pieces such as culverins, matchlocks and the
like. Under the top hung the mainyard,
the sail was reefed and the yard had been
lowered, and it lay at an angle that made me
understand that but little was to be done with
this ship on a bowline. The shrouds, which
were very stout, though scarce one of them
was of the thickness of another, came down
over the side to the channels there, and the
ratlines were all in their places, only that
here again there was great inequality in the
various sizes of the stuff used. There were
iron hoops round the masts, all of them rusty,

cankered, and some of them nearly eaten up.
I looked at the coaming of the hatch, and
observing a splinter, put my hand to it and
found the wood so rotten that methought it
would powder, and I turned the piece about
betwixt my thumb and forefinger, but the
miraculous qualities of the accursed fabric
were in it and iron could not have been more
stubborn to my pinching. The guns, which
I had on the previous night recognised as an
ancient kind of ordnance called sakers, were
as rusty and eaten into as the mast-hoops.

How am I, who have no paint but ink, no
brush but a goose-quill, to convey to you an
idea of the mouldiness and rottenness of this
ship? 'Twas easy to guess why she glowed
at night, when you saw the rail of her bulwarks and marked a rugged unevenness such
as I might liken to the jagged edge you
observe through a telescope in the moon on
the side where the earth's shadow is, as
though time had teeth, indeed, and was for

ever gnawing at these banned and sea-tossed timbers as rats at a floor.

There lay a great hatchway in front of the mainmast covered with tarpaulings, handsomely mended in a score of places. These matters I took in with a sailor's quickness; also that the ship was blowing away to leeward under reefed courses, above which no canvas was shown; also that the foresail and mainsail had a very dingy, collier-like look, and had manifestly been patched and repaired many times over, though whether their capacity of standing to a gale was due to the cloth being stout and substantial still, or because of their endevilment, I could not tell, nor did I like to conjecture. There was no one to be seen, but, as I afterwards found out, that was because the crew were at breakfast below.

I ascended the quarter-deck, and, perceiving Vanderdecken standing on the poop, went up to him, touching my hat as a sailor's

salute ; but the coat I was rigged out in was
so outrageously clumsy and ample, that the
wind, which blew very hard indeed, filling
and distending the skirts of it, was within an
ace of upsetting me, but, happily, a lurch of
the ship swept me towards a mizzen backstay, to which I contrived to cling until I
had recovered my breath and the surprise I
was under.   There was a small house in the
middle of this poop, about ten feet from
where the head of the tiller would come
when amidships, possibly designed for the
convenience of the captain and officers for
making their calculations when in narrow
waters, and for the storing of their marine
instruments, flags and the like.   Be that as
it may, Captain Vanderdecken beckoned
me to it, and under the lee of it the
shelter was such as to enable us to easily
converse.

I looked at him as closely as I durst.   His
eyes were extraordinarily piercing and pas-

sionate, with the cruel brilliance in them such
as may be noticed in the insane ; the lower
part of his face was hidden in hair, but the
skin of as much of it as was visible, for his
cap was dragged low down upon his brows,
was pale, of a haggard sallowness, expressed
best in paintings of the dead where time has
produced the original whiteness of the pig-
ment.   It was impossible that I should have
observed this in him in the mani-coloured
lamplight of the preceding night.   Yet did
not his graveyard complexion detract from
the majesty and imperiousness of his mien
and port.   I could readily conceive that the
defiance of his heart would be hell-like in
obstinacy, and that here was a man whose
pride and passions would qualify him for a
foremost place among the most daring of
those fallen spirits of whom our glorious poet
has written.

He was habited as when I first saw him.
We stood together against this deck-house,

and whilst he remained silent for some
moments, meanwhile keeping his eyes fixed
on me, my gaze went from him to the ship
and the sea around us. It was a thick,
leaden, angry morning; such weather as we
had had a dose of in that storm I wrote about,
and of which forerunners might have been
found on the preceding night in the lightning
in the north-west and in the halo that girdled
the moon. The wind was west-north-west;
the seas had the height and weight you find
in that vast ocean, amid whose hollows we
were driving; 'twas all greyness and a flying
of spumy rain and a heavy roaring coming
from the head of every sea as it arched its
summit for the thunderous downwards rush
that filled the valley at its foot with a boiling
of white water. The sky was a hard leaden
blankness; and whenever there came a break
of faintness amid the seemingly stirless ceiling
of vapour, you would see the scud, thin and
brown, like drainings of smoke from a

chimney-pot, flying with incredible velocity
to the east and south.

But it was the sight of the ancient ship
that rendered the warring ocean so strange a
scene that, had I never before witnessed a
storm at sea, I could not have wondered
more at what I saw.   She was lying to under
her reefed fore and mainsail, surging dead
to leeward on every scend of the billows, and
travelling the faster for the great height of
side she showed.   From time to time a sea
would strike her with a severe shock upon
the bow or the waist, and often curl over in
a mighty hissing and seething, though the
wet quickly poured away overboard through
the ports.   Through the skeleton-iron frame
of what had once been a great poop lantern,
the blast yelled like an imprisoned maniac,
and shook the metal with a sound as of
clanking chains.   The vessel had her topsail
and topgallant-yards aloft, and the sails lay
furled upon them.   The height of her poop,

the depth of her waist, the roundness of her great bulwarked bows, her beak, which I could just catch a glimpse of under her bowsprit, the unequal thickness of the rigging, the indescribable appearance of the sails, the hugeness of the blocks aloft; the whole plunging and rolling amidst the frothing troughs, whilst at the long tiller, the end ornamented with a lion's head, stood a strangely-attired, muffled-up man, grasping a rope wound round the tiller-head, presented such a picture of olden times, made as living as the current moment by the action of the seas, the vitality of the persons I gazed at, the solid substantiality of the aged fabric itself, that the memory of it often chills my brain with fear that I am crazed, and that my experience is but a black and melancholy fancy victorious over my understanding.

And I say would to Heaven this were so, for better that my soul should be racked by a diseased and disordered mind than that I should have suffered the heart-breaking sorrow, the irreparable loss it is my present business to relate in this narrative.

The captain, having inspected me narrowly, asked me how I had slept. I answered "Well," for I was now resolved to present a composed front to this man and his mates, be they and their ship what they would. I had given my nerves play and it was about time I recollected I was an Englishman and a sailor.

"All vessels but mine," said he, in his thrilling, organ-like voice, glancing about him with a scowl, "catch the luck of the wind. Had the weather lingered as it was for another three days, we should have had Agulhas on the beam and the ship's head north-west. 'Tis bitter hard, these encounters of storms, when a few hours of fair wind would blow us round the Cape."

He clenched his hands fiercely, and shot a fiery glance at the windward horizon.

Just then the man styled Herman Van Vogelaar, the mate, arrived, and without taking the least notice of me, said something to the captain, but what, I did not catch; it doubtless referred to some job he had been sent forward to see to. I was greatly struck by the rugged, weather-beaten look of this man; his face in the daylight discovered a mere surface of knobs, and warts, and wrinkles, with a nose the shape of one end of a plantain that has been cut in two, and little, misty eyes, deep in their holes, and surrounded by yellow lashes; his dress was that of a sailor of my own time. But what affected and impressed me even more than did the utter indifference manifested towards my presence by him and by the helmsman—as though, indeed, I was as invisible as the wind—was the pallor underlying the lineaments of this mate. Had I

been asked what would be the complexion of
men dug up from their graves after lying
there, I should have pointed to the countenances of Vanderdecken and Van Vogelaar—
yes, and to Prins and the seaman who
steered.   It was, in truth, as though Captain
Skevington had hit the frightful reality in his
dark and dreadful ideas touching the crew
of this ship being men who presented the
aspect they would have offered at the time of
their death, and who, wearing that death-
bed appearance, were doomed to complete
the sentence passed upon them—no longer
"pensioners on the bounty of an hour," as the
poet Young terms us mortals, but wretches,
rendered supernatural by the impiety of that
fierce but noble figure, whose falcon-flashing
eye looked curses at the gale whilst I
watched him.

The mate left us and went to the helmsman,
by whose side he stood as if conning the ship.
The captain showed no heed of my presence

for a minute or two; when, glancing at me, he said, "'Tis fortunate you speak Dutch, though your pronunciation has a strange sound. For my part, I just know enough of your tongue to hail a ship and to say, 'I will send a boat.' Where did you learn my language?"

"I picked it up during several voyages I made to Rotterdam," I replied.

"Do you know Amsterdam?"

"No, sir," said I.

He mused a little, and then said, "They will think me lost or sunk by the guns of the enemy. Add the long and tedious voyage out to the months which have passed since last July!" he sighed deeply.

"When did you sail from Amsterdam, sir?" I inquired, for I was as particular as he to say "mynheer."

"On the First of November," he answered.

"In what year?" said I.

He cried out, fiercely, "Are your senses

still overboard that you repeat that question ?
Certainly last year—when else ?"

I looked down upon the deck.

" I have reason to remember my passage
through the narrow seas," continued he,
speaking in a softened voice, as though his
sense of courtesy upbraided him. " I sighted
the squadron of your Admiral Ayscue and a
frigate hauled out in chase of me, but the
Braave was too fleet for her, and at dusk
we had sunk the Englishman to his lower
yards!"

As he said this I felt yet again the chill of
a dread I had hoped to vanquish strike upon
my senses like the air of a vault upon the
face. It was impossible that I could now
miss seeing how it was. If this man, together
with his crew, were not endevilled, as Captain
Skevington had surmised, yet it was certain
that life was terminated in him with the Curse
his wickedness had called down upon his ship
and her wretched crew. Existence had come

to a stand in his brain ; with him it was for
ever the year of our Lord 1653 ; time had
been drowned in the eternity of the punishment that had come upon him !

I lifted my startled eyes to Vanderdecken's
face and convulsively clasped my hands,
whilst I thought of the mighty chapter of
history which had been written since his day,
and of the ashes of events prodigious in their
time, and in memory still, which covered—
as do the lava and scoriæ the rocks of some
volcanic-created island—the years from the
hour of his doom down to the moment of our
meeting.   The peace of 1654—the later war
of 1665—Ruyter at Sheerness and Chatham
and in the Hope—a stadtholder of Vanderdecken's country becoming a King of England
—the peace of Ryswick—Malplaquet—the
semi-Gallican founding of the Batavian Republic — with how much more that my
memory did not carry ? All as non-existent
to this man at my side as to any human

creature who had died at the hour when the
Death Ship sailed on her last passage home
from the island of Java!

CHAPTER XVI.

VANDERDECKEN SHOWS ME HIS PRESENT
FOR LITTLE MARGARETHA.

AT this moment Prins stepped on to the poop, and informed the captain that break-fast was ready.

"Sir," said Vanderdecken to me, with a courtesy that I guessed to be as capricious as his passion, "you will have feared I meant to starve you."

"No, mynheer," I replied.

"You will find our fare poor," he con-tinued. "Be pleased to follow me."

"Sir," said I, "forgive me if I detain you for an instant. I am too sensible of your kindness not to desire that you will enable me to merit it by serving you in the navigation of this ship in any capacity you choose to name, until we meet with a vessel that shall rid you of my presence."

"You appear to have but a poor opinion of us Dutch," said he, still speaking with courtesy; "be pleased to know that a Hollander is never happier than in relieving distress. But come, sir, the shelter of the cabin will be grateful to you after this stormy deck."

I said no more, and gathering the flapping skirts of the coat on me to my side, that the gale might not sweep me off my legs, I followed him into the cabin under the poop, marvelling, as I went, at the miracle wrought on behalf of this ship, that her hold should still yield provisions and water for her crew after a century-and-a-half of use.

Now you will have deemed by this time that I had supped full enough of surprises. But conceive of my astonishment on entering the cabin, that was less darksome than I

should have conceived it, on seeing a girl of
from eighteen to twenty years of age, seated
at the table on the right hand of the captain's
chair !

I came to a stand, struck motionless with
astonishment ; whilst she, uttering an exclamation of surprise, hastily rose and stood staring at me, leaning with her right hand on the
table to steady herself. It was as certain that
she had been as ignorant of my presence on
board as I, to this instant, of her existence.
The thought that instantly flashed upon me
was that she was Vanderdecken's daughter,
that the Curse that had fallen on the ship
included her, as it had all others of the vessel's
miserable company of men, and that in con-
sonance with Captain Skevington's mad but
astonishing theory, touching the people of this
Death Ship, she discovered the appearance
she would have presented at the hour of her
death, though vitalised in that aspect by the
sentence that kept the Braave afloat and her

people quick and sentient. I was the more willing to suppose this by her apparel, which was of the kind I had seen in old Dutch paintings at Rotterdam, for it consisted of a black velvet jacket, very beautifully fitting her figure, trimmed with fur and enriched with many small golden buttons ; a green silk gown, plain and very full, as though made for a bigger woman. There was a rope of pearls round her neck, and I spied a diamond of great splendour blazing on the forefinger of the hand on which she leaned. She wore small red shoes and her hair was undressed.

Observation and the power of comprehending what one sees are rapid, otherwise it would have been impossible for me to have mastered the details I have set before you in the short time that intervened between my entering the cabin and seating myself at the table. Yet, short as that time was, it enabled me to witness in this girl such sweetness, fairness and loveliness of face as I vow no

man could conceive the truth of who had not
beheld it with his own eyes. 'Tis an old
poet who writes of " the still harmony, whose
diapason lies within a brow," and of the
" sweet silent rhetorick of persuading eyes,"
and another more delicately choice yet in
fancy, of

> " The daintie touch,
> The tender flesh, the colour bright, and such
> As Parians see in marble, skin more fair,
> More glorious head and far more glorious hair ;
> Eyes full of grace and quickness, purer roses——"

but of this beauty, shining sun-like in that
labouring ancient cabin, gazing at me half-
wistful, half-amazed, with an inclined posture
of her form as though she would on a sudden
race to greet me, what could the noblest poet
of them all sing, only to tell of the soft violet
of her eyes, of her hair of dusky gold, self-
luminous as though the gilding light of a
ruddy beam of sunset lingered amid the thick
abundant tresses heedlessly knotted with a
riband a little lower than the line of the

ears, thence falling in a bright loose shower down her back, whilst over her forehead, white as though wrought out of the sea foam, the gilded curls were gathered in a shadow only a little darker than amber.

All this I saw and more yet, for whilst I stood looking at her the mate of the ship, Van Vogelaar, arrived, and both he and the captain, and the man Prins, turning their faces towards me, the warmth, the life of her skin, the living reality of her surprise, the redness of her lips, the diamond glance of her eyes, were so defined by the paleness, the deathly hue, of the flesh of the men's skin, that the fear that she was of this doomed company fell from me, and I knew that I was face to face with one that was mortal like myself.

The captain pointed to the bench on his left hand. I approached the table, giving the girl a low bow before sitting. She curtsied and resumed her seat, but all the while looking at me with an astonishment that greatly heightened her beauty; nor could I fail to see by the slight, but visible changes in the expression of her mouth, that my presence was putting a pleasure in her that grew as perception of my actuality sharpened in her mind.

A coarse, but clean cloth, that was a kind of duck or drill, covered the table, and upon it were a couple of dishes of cold meat, a dish of dried fish, another of dried plantains, a jar of marmalade, and a plate of a singular sort of cakes—yellow and heavy—resembling the crumb of newly-baked bread. These things were kept in their places by a rude framework of wood set upon the table and lashed to it underneath. Before each person there stood a silver cup—one of one design and size, another of another; also an earthen plate, of a grey colour, of Chinese baking, and of the kind exported years since in great quantities from Batavia; and a knife and fork

of a pattern I had never before seen. On our
seating ourselves, Prins went round the table
with two jars—one holding a spirit, which I
afterwards found was a kind of gin, and the
other cold water, with which he manufactured
a bumper for us three men, but the girl drank
the water plain.

Not a word was said whilst Prins was at
this work. As he was filling my cup, the
clock over the door struck eight, the skeleton
appearing and flourishing his lance as before,
and scarce was this ended when the parrot
croaked out, "ひy ʒyn al Verdoomd." I had
forgotten this bird, and the harsh utterance
and dreadful words coming upon me unawares
so startled me that I half-sprang to my feet.
The girl looked down on the table with a
sad face, whilst Vanderdecken said, "'Tis the
clock that excites that fowl ; we shall have to
hang her out of hearing of it."

He never offered to make me known to
the fair creature opposite, but that did not

signify, for, after stealing several peeps at me, she asked in Dutch, but with the artless manner of a child, and in a sweet voice, if I was a Hollander.

I answered, "No, I am an Englishman, madam," feeling the blood warm in my face through the mere speaking with so delicate a beauty.

"I, too, am English!" she cried, in our own tongue.

"Indeed!" I exclaimed, transported out of myself by hearing this, and by perceiving how warm, real and living she was. "But, in the name of Heaven, how is it that you are alone upon this strange ship, amid these mysterious men?" for that question I could no more forbear asking right out than I could conceal the admiration in my eyes, whilst I felt no diffidence in talking, as I made no doubt the English language was unintelligible to the others.

She swiftly glanced at me, but did not

answer. I took this as a hint, and was silent. And yet it did not seem that Vanderdecken or Van Vogelaar heeded us. They appeared as men sunk in deep abstraction, even whilst they ate and drank. Some meat was put before me; Prins offered me a cake, and, being hard set, I fell to. I found the meat salt, but sweet and tender enough, and turning to the mate asked him what it was.

"Antelope," he replied, "yonder," pointing to the other dish, "is buffalo."

"Sir," exclaimed Vanderdecken, with a wonderful stateliness in his manner, "be pleased to despise ceremony here. Such as our fare is, you are welcome. Take as you may require, and Prins will fill your cup as often as you need."

I bowed and thanked him.

"The wind blows hard, Imogene," said he, addressing the girl. "It storms directly along the path we would take. It is miserable," he continued, turning to me, "that a change of weather should come upon us just about those parts where the breeze freshened into this gale last night. But we'll force her to windward yet—hey, Herman?— though—though——" he looked at the lady he had named Imogene and halted abruptly in his speech, but I noticed he could not quickly clear his face of the passionate mad look that darkened it, though it did not qualify the paleness of the skin, but was like the shadow of a heavy storm-cloud passing over the upward-gazing features of a dead man.

The countenances of the mate and Prins darkened to his savage mood. May Heaven pardon me for the thought, but when I considered the bitter vexation of a head wind, and how this vessel was being blown dead away to leeward faster than any line-of-battle ship hove-to, I could not but secretly feel a sailor's sympathy with these unhappy persons, though that this would have been the case had Vanderdecken expressed with his tongue the fearful thoughts which he looked with his eyes I do not think possible, if I know myself at all.

There fell a silence among us, through which we could hear the dreary howling of the wind, the falls of heavy masses of water upon the decks, and the lamentable complaining of the whole fabric, though as these noises were chiefly in the hold the notes rose somewhat dulled. Presently, feeling it indecorus in me to sit silent, I asked the captain what his cargo was.

He answered, "We have much wrought and raw silk, and cloves, musk, nutmegs, mace and pepper, wood for dyeing, drugs, calicoes, lacker-ware and such commodities, sir."

" And how many of a crew, sir?"

Van Vogelaar turned to look at me.

" Ask no questions," exclaimed the girl in English. " You will be misunderstood."

"Our guns are few, but the Braave is a swift ship," said the mate, with a very stern and sullen expression on his rugged face. "She has outsailed one English frigate, and by this time our Admirals should have left us little to fear from the fleets of your Cromwell."

"Pray," said the lady, addressing Vanderdecken, and glancing in like a sunbeam upon this sudden darkness of temper, "tell me of this gentleman—how it happens he is here; I find he is my countryman. Converse with me about him."

If it were possible for human affection to touch into softness the fierce majestic countenance of the noble looking being, whose mien as he sate at the table might have been that of some dethroned emperor, with the pride of Lucifer to sustain him, I might seem to have witnessed the tenderness of it in his ashen, bearded face when he turned the cold glitter of his eyes upon the girl.

"We spoke his ship late last night, when

thou wast asleep, Imogene, and Van Vogelaar
went in our boat to buy tobacco, if they were
willing to sell, but on seeing the boat they
fired upon her. A light air blew, and the
ship moved away. Our boat was returning,
when she spied this gentleman fast drowning.
Van Vogelaar dragged him out of the water,
and—here he is!" saluting me with a grave
inclination of the head.

"Had we changed places," said the stormy-
minded, rugged mate, "what would have
been my fate?"

A colour flashed into Imogene's face, and
she cried, "Oh, Herr Van Vogelaar, your
pardon, if you please. English seamen are
as humane as they are brave."

"Yes," said the mate, with a sneer that
rendered his ugliness quite horrible with the
distortion of it, "because English sailors are
brave they fire upon an inoffensive boat, and
because they are humane they leave their
comrade to perish!"

"Madam," said I, softly, "the character of this ship was known to us."

She slightly raised her eyes, and such a sadness came into them that I feared to see her shed tears. Meanwhile, Vanderdecken had his gaze fixed upon me. He seemed to be musing upon what the mate had said.

"It was your Commodore Young," said he, in his resonant voice, that, to be sure, sounded grandly after the harsh pipes of the mate, "who provoked us. Why should your nation exact the honour of the flag? Has it bred greater seamen than Holland? There is my friend Willem Schouten—many a pipe, when I was a young man, have I smoked with him in his summer-house at Hoorn. Does even your Drake surpass Schouten? No, no! It was not for England to be mistress of the seas!" he exclaimed, with a solemn shake of the head, not wanting in a grave kind of urbanity.

I caught a glance from the girl, but I

needed no hint to keep my tongue still. 'Twas maddening and terrifying enough to hear this man speak of Schouten as a friend —Schouten, who greatly headed the grand procession of mariners such as Dampier, Byron, Anson, and many others who, since his day, have sailed round that Cape Horn— which the stout Hollander was the first to pass and to name—into the great South Sea.

And yet, spite of the effect produced upon me by this man's speech and references, I was sensible of a distinct pricking of my conscience by my patriotism. To hear England sneered at by the natives of a country which has been described by a poet that flourished in the days of Blake and Tromp as the "offscouring of the British sand," and as the "undigested vomit of the sea," was by no means to my liking. But to remonstrate would have been but a mere warring with the dead.

The captain appeared to delight to talk of

the war between the Dutch and the English.
I remember that he praised our Commodore
Bodley, and said that if the States' ambas-
sador, Adrian Paaw, had been a person of
understanding, the treaty might have stood.
This I recollect, but very little more, for, to
be plain, it was not only a frightful thing to
listen to him, but my thoughts were thrown
into the utmost confusion by the loveliness of
the lady who confronted me—by the assurance of the sweet eyes, warm colour, and her
maidenly youth, which lived in every movement, word, smile, or sad look of hers, that
she was no true member of the unholy
and fearful company she lived amongst; by
my wondering how she came to be in this
Death Ship, and how it happened that she
was finely dressed; not to speak of other
speculations, such as how the food upon the
table was provided, and by what means this
ship, which I knew had been struggling
against the will of the Omnipotent for hard

upon one hundred and fifty years, should be supplied with a liberal stock of the conveniences of life.

But we had now done eating. The mate rose and quitted the table, but his place was shortly afterwards taken by another man whom I had not before seen, the second mate as I afterwards discovered, named Antony Arents. This person looked to be about fifty years of age. He wore high boots and a cloak and a soft flapping hat, which he threw down on entering. His left eye had a cast and the bridge of his nose was broken, but his countenance was of the true Dutch character, and in some points he was like the boatswain, Antony Jans, whom I had seen on deck when waking into consciousness, only that he had less flesh to his belly. But in him was the same ghastly hue of skin you saw in the others; 'twas in his hands as in his face; had you come across him in his sleep you would have said he had been dead some days. And, indeed, never did I view a corpse made ready for casting overboard that had the aspect of the dead so strong upon it as these men. He helped himself to food, taking not the least notice of me.

Prins meanwhile had put a box of tobacco and some long clay pipes upon the table, one of which Vanderdecken took and filled, asking me to smoke. I thanked him, wondering what sort of tobacco time had converted this weed into, took the tinder-box from the captain and lighted my pipe. Well, if this was an ancient tobacco age had not spoilt its qualities. It smoked very sweet and sound.

" We are on short allowance," said the captain. " Our stock has run low. It will be a hardship if we should come to want tobacco."

I made no reply, being determined to learn all I could about this ship and her people from Miss Imogene before offering suggestions, for though there is no living man whose nose I would not offer to stroke for calling me a coward, yet I am not ashamed to say this Captain Vanderdecken terrified me and I feared his wrath.

The girl, with her elbows on the table and her fair chin resting on her hands, which made an ivory cup for her face, watched me continuously with eyes whose brightness the large and sparkling diamond on her forefinger did not match by many degrees of glory.

"Are you long from England?" says she to me presently in Dutch, that Vanderdecken might know what we talked about.

"We sailed in April last," I replied. "And you, madam?"

She either did not hear the question or would not answer.

"Are you married?" asked the captain of me, smoking very slowly to get the true relish of the tobacco, whilst the second mate chewed his food with vacant eyes, squinting straight ahead or meeting in a traverse on his plate.

"No, sir," I replied.

"Are your parents living?" he said.

"My mother is alive," I answered.

"Ah!" said he, speaking as one in a reverie, "A sailor should not marry. What is more uncertain than the sea? The mariner's wife can never make sure of her husband's return. What will mine be thinking if we continue to be blown back as we are now by these westerly gales? It seems longer than months, yea, it appears to me to be years, since I last beheld her and my daughters standing near the Schreyerstoren, weeping and waving their farewells to me. My eldest girl, Geertruida, will be grown sick at heart with her long yearning for the parcel of silk I have for her. And Margaretha——" he sighed, softly. Then turning to Imogene, he said, "My dear, show this gentleman the toy I am taking home for my little Margaretha."

She rose with a look of pain in her face, and stepped to the cabin that was next the captain's. I now understood why he had desired me to speak in subdued tones last night, for that was the room in which she slept. The ease with which she moved upon that heaving deck was wonderful, and this verse of a ballad came into my head as I watched her go from the table to her cabin—

"No form he saw of mortal mould,
   It shone like ocean's snowy foam;
Her ringlets waved in living gold,
   Her mirror crystal, pearl her comb."

Ay, the ocean might have owned her for a child, with such dainty, elegant ease did she accommodate her form to the sweep and heave of its billows, as denoted by the motions of the ship; as some lovely gull with breast of snowy down and wings of ermine airily expresses the swing and charge of the surge by its manner of falling in each hollow and lifting above each head on outstretched pinion. Her costume too, that was so strange a thing,

giving to this interior so romantic an appearance that, had the ship been still and you had
looked in at the cabin door, then, with this
lady's beauty and dress, the majestic figure of
Vanderdecken smoking in his high-backed
chair, the second mate at his food, Prins
standing like one that dreams, all the faces
but the girl's and mine ghastly, the strange
beauty of the lamp that swung over the table,
the oval frames holding paintings so bleared
and dusky that it was difficult to make out
the subjects, the dim and wasted colour of the
cabin walls, and the bald tawdriness of what
had been rich giltwork, the clock of ancient
pattern, the parrot cage—I say, had you been
brought on a sudden to view this interior
from the door, you might have easily deemed
it some large astonishing picture painted
to the very height of the greatest master's
perfection.

In a moment or two Miss Imogene returned, and coming to the table placed upon

it a little figure about five inches tall. It was of some metal and had been gaily coloured as I supposed from what was left of the old tints. Its style was a red cloak falling down its back, a small cap with a feather, shoes almost hidden with great rosettes, hose as high as the thigh, and then a sort of blouse with a girdle. Both arms hung before in a very easy and natural posture and the hands grasped a flute.

Vanderdecken, putting down his pipe, took a key from under the cloak of the figure and wound the automaton up as a clock, when it instantly lifted the flute to its mouth, in the exact manner of life, and played a tune. The sound was very pure though piercing, the melody simple and flowing. In all, the figure played six tunes without any sound of the clock-work within, and it was undoubtedly a very curious and costly toy.

The second mate stalked out in the middle of this performance, having finished his meal, and showing no more sensibility to what was doing than did the table the figure played on. The eyes of the man Prins had a sickly, far-away look, to be imagined only, for no one could describe it. Vanderdecken lighted his pipe when the automaton struck up, and nodded gravely to the fluting with as much pleasure in his face as so fierce and haughty a countenance could express. The girl stood leaning upon the table, with a listlessness in her manner and constantly regarding me.

Scarce had the sixth tune been played, when the parrot called out from his cage, "Wy zyn al Verdomd!" clearly showing that she knew when the entertainment was over. Her pronouncing these words in Dutch robbed them somewhat, to my ear, of their tremendous import, but still it was a terrible sentence for the creature to have lighted on, and I wondered what her age was, for she could not have been newly-hatched when Vanderdecken bought her, as—he had told me—she then spoke the same words. However, the captain was full of his flute-player, and neither he nor Imogene noticed the parrot.

"This should delight my little Margaretha," said he, lifting the figure and examining it ; "'tis as cunning a toy as ever I saw. I bought it at Batavia, from an old friend of mine, Meeuves Meindertszoom Bakker, who had purchased it of a sailor belonging to the company's ship, Revolutie, for eight ducats. 'Twill rejoice my child ; you shall present it to her, Imogene. I would not sell it for five hundred dollars ; 'tis worthy to be John Muller's work."

He ceased speaking, lifting his hand ; then exclaimed, "Hark! how the wind continues to storm."

He gave the figure to the girl who returned it to her cabin.

In a few minutes he put down his pipe and

bade Prins bring him his skin or fur cap, and
then rose, impressing me as keenly as though
I viewed him for the first time by the nobility
of his stature, his great beard flowing to the
waist, the sharp supernatural fires in his eyes
as if the light there were living flames.   In
silence he quitted the cabin, acting like a man
influenced by spells, without the governance
of the logic of human behaviour.

CHAPTER XVII.

BEING in the way now of enjoying a talk with Imogene, the ridiculousness of the dress I was in struck me, and I asked Prins, who was clearing the table, whether my own clothes were yet dry. He answered they were hung up in the furnace near the cookhouse, by which I suppose he meant the caboose, and that when they were dry he would bring them to my cabin.

"In these things," said I, addressing Imogene in English, whilst I turned my head about to catch a sight of my tails, "I feel like a fool in a carnival. What ages this garb represents I cannot conceive, but it surely does not represent less than a century of fashion."

"And what must you think of my attire?" said she, seating herself in the captain's chair, which her beauty made a throne of in a breath, the light of her hair gilding it. "But all things are wonderful here," she added, with a half-glance at Prins, whose movements and manner as he removed the dishes from the table were as deaf and soulless as the behaviour of the figure that had just piped to us. "You know, of course, what ship this is?"

I said "Yes," in a subdued voice, and sat down on the end of the bench near her, adding, "Will the captain take it amiss if we converse?"

"No," she answered, "but should he forbid it and then find you speaking to me, his temper would be dreadful. He is a terribly passionate man. Yet he is gentle to me, and speaks of his wife and children with exquisite tenderness."

" His wife and children!   God help him!"

"Oh!" she cried, trembling, "I cannot express to you the horror and pain I feel when I hear him talk of them as though he should find them as they were—altered by the length of a year only—when he parted from them.   He does not know that he is cursed — none of them on board this ship know it of themselves."

" Is that so?" I exclaimed.   "Surely their repeated failures to pass the Agulhas point must convince them that the will of God is opposed to their attempts and that they are doomed men."

She leaned her fair cheek upon her hand with a thoughtful absent expression in her violet eyes, though they remained fixed upon me with a child-like simplicity extraordinarily fascinating.   I particularly noticed the beautiful turn of her wrist, the fairy delicacy of her nostrils and mouth, and the enchanting curve of her chin to her throat.   Her figure was full, and in the swell of her breasts and the breadth of her shoulders, fining down into a waist in admirable harmony with her stature and make, you might seem to have witnessed every assurance of robustness. But you found a suggestion rather than a character of fragility in the beauty of her face that caused the very delight you took in the gold and lilies and violets of her loveliness to grow pensive. There was a complete absence of embarrassment in her manner towards me.

" If you please, what name am I to know you by ?" she asked.

"Geoffrey Fenton," I answered, "and you ?"

" Imogene Dudley." I bowed to her, and she continued, " Are you a sailor ?"

I raised my hands half-mockingly, and said, " Do I not look my calling ?" but recollecting my apparel, I burst into a laugh and exclaimed, touching the faded finery upon the cuff of my coat, " You will have thought me a beadle or a footman."

She shook her head smiling, but instantly grew grave, and now spoke in a most earnest voice. " I will tell you all I know about this ship and about myself. My father was Captain Dudley, of Portsmouth, and nearly five years ago, as closely as I can reckon time where time has ceased to all the others, he commanded a ship named the Flying Fish, and took me and my mother with him on a voyage to China. We called at Table Bay, but when we were off the coast where Algoa Bay is situated, the ship was set on fire by one of the crew entering the hold with a lighted candle and attempting to steal some rum. The flames quickly raged, the ship was not to be saved, the boats were lowered and my mother and I and a seaman entered one of them, but suddenly the ship blew up, destroying the boats that were against its side, and when the smoke cleared off nothing was to be seen on the water but a few pieces of blackened timber. Our boat had been saved by my father ordering the man to keep her at a good distance lest a panic arose and she should be entered by too great a number. The shock so affected my mother that she lost her mind." Here Imogene hid her face. When she looked at me again her face was wet, nevertheless she continued : "She died on the night following the loss of the ship, and I was left alone with the sailor. We were many leagues from the land, we had no sail, the oars were heavy. I was too weak and ill to help him with them, and the fierce heat soon melted the strength out of him, so that he left off rowing. He was good to me, gentle and very sorrowful about me. I cried so much over losing my father and mother, and at our dreadful situation, that I thought my heart would break, and I prayed that it might, for indeed I wanted to die." She drew a deep hysteric breath, tremulous as a long bitter sob. "We drifted here and there for five days, after which thirst and hunger bereft me of my senses, and I remember no more till I awoke in this ship. I then learnt that they had passed our boat close, and had stopped the vessel to inspect her. The seaman was dead, and they supposed me dead too, but Captain Vanderdecken, fancying a likeness in me to his daughter Alida, called to his men to bring me on board. They did so and found life in me."

"And you have been in this vessel ever since!" cried I.

"Ever since!" she responded.

"That is to say," I exclaimed, scarcely realising the truth, "for hard upon five years!"

She hid her eyes and shook her sweet face in the cover of her hands, as if she could not bear to think of it. I waited a little, partly that she might have time to recover her tranquillity, and partly that Prins might make an

end of his business and go, though, let me
declare, he gave us no more heed than had
he been the clock ; much less, indeed, than
did the parrot that, having rounded her head,
after the manner of those birds, till her beak
was uppermost, watched us with the broadside of her face, and therefore with one eye,
with horrid pertinacity and gravity.

"But can it be, Miss Dudley," said I,
"that Captain Vanderdecken never intends
to part with you ?"

She looked up quickly, and said, "My
position is incredibly strange. He has a
father's fondness for me, and declares that,
as I have no relations, I shall be one of his
children, and live with his wife and daughters
at Amsterdam. But he has no sense of time.
Neither he nor the miserable crew can compute. To him and the others this is the year
1654, and he supposes that he sailed from
Batavia in July of last year, that is, as he
conceives, in 1653. At first I tried to make

him understand what century this was, but
he patted my cheek, and said my senses had
not returned, and, when I persisted, he grew
angry, and his temper so terrified me that I
feigned to agree with him, and have ever
since done so."

I reflected, and said, " It must be as you
say, and as I have already noted ; for, did
the Almighty grant him and his crew any
perception of the passage of time, is it conceivable that he would talk of his wife and
children as still living, and be eager to return
to them ?   When did you discover that this
was the Phantom Ship ?"

" I had heard that there was such a vessel
from my father, and when Captain Vanderdecken talked to me and I marked the
colour of his face and the appearance of the
crew, and the glow that shone upon the
vessel in the dark, with other strange things,
such as her ancient appearance, I soon satisfied myself."

"Father of Mercy!" I cried, "what a situation for a young girl!"

"When I felt sure of the ship," she said, "I should have drowned myself in my misery and terror, only I dreaded God's wrath. I felt that if I humbly resigned myself to His Holy Will He would suffer the spirits of my father and mother to be with me and watch over me. But, oh! what a tedious waiting has it been, what bitter weariness of sea and sky! Again and again have I entreated Captain Vanderdecken to put me on board some passing ship, but not conceiving of the years which run by, and every tempest that obstructs him melting as a memory into the last, so that the rebuffs of a century past are to him as forgotten things, or possessing the same sort of recentness that in a day or two this gale, which is now blowing, will have, he thinks to encourage me by saying that next time he is certain to round the headland, that, as he has adopted, so he must not part with me, but carry me in his own ship and under his own protection to his wife and home."

I understood her and admired the cleverness with which she rendered intelligible to me the state of mind of the captain and crew of this ship, that is to say so far as concerned their incapacity to compute the passage of the days. For is it not evident that if these men knew that they were doomed never to round the Cape, they would cease striving to do so? And would they not long ago have understood the character of the Judgment that had been passed upon them had they been permitted to comprehend that year after year rolled on, ay, even into centuries, and still found them beaten back regularly from the same part of the ocean to the passing of which their struggles had been directed? How far memory in them was suffered to go back so as to count the number of times they were driven afresh to the eastwards, I could not imagine; but no doubt Imogene, who knew Vanderdecken well, was right when she said that the recollection of the last rebuff melted into every present one, so that, in short, in this respect they were as men without memory. And this must have been so, for they worked with hope; whereas hope would have long since died in them could they have recollected.

"What are your thoughts," I asked her, "as regards their mortality? Are they human?"

"Yes, Mr. Fenton, they must be human, for they think of their homes and wives and children," she replied.

I was struck with this, though I said, "Might not their very yearning be a part of the Curse? For if you extinguish their desire of getting home, the impulse that keeps them striving with the elements would disappear, and they would say, 'Since we cannot get westwards and so to Europe, we'll head for the east and make for the Indies?'"

" It is a thing impossible to reason upon," she exclaimed, sadly, and pressing her hand to her brow. " The Great God here, in this ship, has worked in miracles and mysteries for purposes of His own. Who can explain His ways? Sometimes I have thought by the dreadful hue of the skin of their faces that they are men dead in body, but forced into the behaviour of living beings by the strength of the Curse that works in them."

I replied that in saying this she had exactly hit upon the fancy of my late captain, who had taken his own life on the previous evening, which fancy now struck me as an amazing inspiration, seeing that it was her own opinion and that my own judgment fully concurred in it.

" 'Tis impossible," said she, " that they can be as we are. They are supernaturally alive. Oh! it is shocking to think of. Is it not wonderful that my long association with these people has not driven me mad? Yet

the captain loves me as a father; such is his
tenderness at times when he talks of his
home and strives to keep up my heart by
warranting that next time—it is always next
time—we shall pass the Cape and all will be
well with us, that I am lost in wonder he
could have ever so acted as to bring the curse
of an eternal life of hopeless struggle upon
him and his men."

"Ay," cried I, "and why should his men
be accursed?"

"I have often asked myself that whilst
watching them," she replied. "But then I
have answered, why should innocent little
children bear in their forms, and in their
minds too, the diseases and infirmities caused
by the wickedness and recklessness of persons, perhaps several generations removed
from them? We dare not question—'tis
impious, Mr. Fenton. In this ship especially
must we be as mute spectators only, for we
are two living persons standing amid shadows,

and viewing so marvellous a mystery that I tremble to the depth of my soul at the thoughts of my nearness to the Majesty of an offended God!"

By this time Prins had quitted the cabin, and the girl and I were alone.   There was a great weight of sea running, and the rolling of the ship was very violent.   This end of the vessel was so tall that it rose buoyant from the head of every billow that leapt at her afterpart ; but the thunder of the seas smiting her in the waist would roar like a tempest through the ship ; you could hear the waters washing about the deck there ; then the groaning and complaining below was continuous, and the sounds which pene- trated the cabin from the gale in the rigging made you think of the affrighted bellowing of bulls chased by wolves in full cry.

" There seems to be a fierce storm blow- ing," said Imogene, who had watched my face whilst I listened ; " but since I have

been in this ship there have been far wilder
tempests than this."

"No doubt, in all the weary years you
have spent here. What has been your experience of the winds which regularly oppose
the ship? Do they happen naturally, as in
the case of this one, which was plentifully
betokened by the look of the moon and other
signs, or do they rise on a sudden—in such
wise, I mean, as would make one see they
were for this vessel only, and are a temporary
change in the laws of nature hereabouts that
the Curse may be continued?"

"I cannot answer; all that I can speak to
is this : as punctually as we arrive at a given
place the wind heads us, as used to be my
poor father's term and as all seamen say.
And sometimes it blows softly and sometimes
it rises into fury. But let it come as it will
the vessel is blown or driven back a great
many leagues, but how far I cannot say, for
Vanderdecken himself does not know."

I would not trouble her with further questions touching what I will call the nautical routine of the ship and the manœuvring of the unhappy creatures the vessel carried, because already I suspected that I should have rather more leisure than I should relish to look into these matters myself. But as she manifestly took a pleasure in conversing with me, and as I wished to obtain all the information possible about this Death Ship, and as, should Vanderdecken forbid my associating with or addressing her, there might be no one else on board of whom I could venture to make inquiries, I determined at once to push my researches as far as courtesy permitted.

"I trust, Miss Dudley," said I, finding a singular delight in the pure virginal resting of her violet eyes, sparkling like the jewels of a crown, on mine as I talked to her, "that my questions do not tease you——"

"Oh, no!" she interrupted. "If you but

knew how glad I am, how it gives me fresh heart to hear you speak, to see your living face after my long desolating communion with the people of this ship!"

"Indeed I can conceive it!" said I. "May God grant that what I viewed last night as a most dreadful misfortune, full of terror, ay, even to madness, may prove the greatest stroke of good luck that could have befallen me. But of what is to be done we must talk later on. I shall require to look about me. Tell me now, madam, if you will, how is this ship provisioned? Surely these men are not miraculously fed; and 'tis certain that the meat I tasted this morning has been cured since 1653!"

She smiled and said, "When they run short of food or water they sail for some part of the coast where there is a river. There they go on shore in boats, armed with muskets, and come off with all that they can kill."

"Ha!" cried I, fetching a deep breath, "there is some plain sailing in this unholy business after all. But how do they manage for ammunition? Surely they must long ago have expended their original stock?"

"I can but guess. About a twelvemonth ago we met with an abandoned ship, out of which Vanderdecken conveyed a great quantity of tobacco, powder, money and articles of food, a few cases of marmalade and some barrels of flour. Whether these shipwrecked vessels are left lying upon the sea for him to take provisions from by the Power that has sentenced him to his fearful fate I cannot say, but since I have been in this vessel we have fallen in with three deserted ships, both floating and ashore on the coast, and this may have been their method throughout of providing themselves with what they needed, backed by such further food as I have never known them to miss of with their muskets and fowling-pieces."

"So!" cried I, greatly marvelling. "Now I understand how it happens that the captain can lend me such latter-day clothes as these from his seventeenth-century wardrobe, and that you—forgive me, madam—are attired as I see you."

She answered, "In their hold they have a great quantity of silks and materials for making gowns for women. This jacket," said she, meaning that which she was wearing, "is one article out of several chests of clothes Captain Vanderdecken was carrying home for his wife and daughters and friends. Do you notice the style, Mr. Fenton?" she added, turning about her full and graceful figure that I might see the jacket, "it is certainly of the last century. In the captain's cabin is the portrait of one of his daughters dressed in much the same way.

"You, at all events," said I, "are not likely to run short of clothes."

"Oh!" she answered, with a toss of her head, half of weariness, half of scorn as it seemed to me, "there is a chest in my cabin full of clothes fit for the grandest Duchess in England. I use such as come most readily to my hands. What need have I," she exclaimed, pushing her hair from her forehead, "to care whether the colours I take match, or whether the gown is too full. This jacket fits me as do all the clothes that were intended for Geertruida Vanderdecken." Then, noticing my eyes resting on the pearls, she said, taking the beautiful and costly rope in her hands, "There is a great stock of finery of this kind in the ship. About a fortnight or three weeks after I had been rescued, the captain ordered Prins to bring a large case into the cabin; it was put upon the table and the captain opened it. 'Twas like a jeweller's shop in miniature, containing several divi-

sions, one full of pearl ornaments, another of
rings, of which he bid me choose one to wear,
and I took this," holding up her forefinger
whereon the jewel blazed, "a third of ear-
rings and many other trinkets ; some, as I
should fancy, more ancient than this ship,
others of a later time.   How he got much of
this treasure I know."

"How?" asked I, deeply interested.

"Well," said she, letting fall the pearls
around her neck to toy with the ring, "a fair
proportion he had purchased for a merchant
of Amsterdam ; chiefly eastern jewellery that
had made its way from Indian cities to Java ;
other parcels he was taking home on his own
account ; but much of it, too, along with a
store of further treasure—some of which I
have seen, and which consists of virgin silver,
bars of gold, coated with pewter to deceive
the pirates and buccaneers, candlesticks and
crucifixes of precious metal—he found in the
wreck of a great Spanish ship which lay

abandoned and going to pieces on a shoal
off the coast of Natal.   This happened during
his progress from Batavia to the Cape, before
he was cursed, and therefore it falls within his
memory.   What other treasure there is, his
men have no doubt brought away from the
wrecked vessels they have examined for food,
powder and the like, during the years they
have been sailing about this ocean."

"So," cried I, lost in amazement by what I
heard, "it is in this fashion that the Phantom
Ship supplies her wants.   As ships grow
more numerous, her opportunities will in-
crease, for 'tis terrible to think of the number of vessels which go a-missing ; and,
besides, this is the road to India, along which
pass the most richly freighted of Europe's
merchant fleets.   Now I understand how
Vanderdecken manages to keep his crew
supplied with clothes, and his ship with sails
and cordage.   But, Lord !" cried I, "if there
be nothing magical in this, yet surely the

the Evil Spirit must be suffered to have a hand in the keeping of the bones of this old fabric together!"

As I said this, Prins entered the cabin, and said, shortly, "Your clothes are dry, mynheer; they are below."

On which Imogene rose, and giving me a bow, went to her own cabin.

CHAPTER XVIII.

THE DEATH SHIP MUST BE SLOW AT PLYING.

I stood a moment or two at the door watching the clock whilst it struck, and greatly admiring the workmanship of the skeleton that rose and speared with his lance, keeping time to the sonorous chiming, which sang with a solemn interval between each beat. The great age of this time-keeper was beyond question, but the horn that protected the face of it prevented me from perceiving if there was any maker's name or date there.

As the skeleton sank, I could not but admire the patness of the mechanism to the condition of the ship and her crew, for what could surpass the irony of this representation of Death perpetually foiled in his efforts to

slay Time, which was yet the case of Vanderdecken and his men, whose mortality was
constrained to an endless triumph over that
force which drives all men born of woman
through Nature into Eternity.

The parrot hanging near, I stayed yet to
look at her and then spoke to the creature in
my rugged Dutch, but to no purpose; with
the slow motion of her kind she contorted
herself until, with her beak uppermost, she
brought her larboard eye to bear full upon
me; and so fixed and unwinking was her
stare that I greatly disliked it, nay, felt that
if I lingered I should fear it, and was going
when she brought me to a stand by a hollow
" Ha! ha! ha!" just such a note as fancy
would give to the ghost of a Dutchman, who
had been large, fat and guttural when alive,
could the spectre of such a one laugh in his
coffin or in a vault. The age which this bird
had attained made her mere appearance chill-
ing to the blood, though I am aware these

creatures are long-lived and that no man with certainty could say they might not flourish two hundred years and more. She was not bald. All her feathers were sound and smooth. Yet, as I made my way to my cabin, it terrified me into downright despondency to conceive of this parrot sharing in the Curse that Vanderdecken had provoked. For if this soulless fowl could be involved in the general fate merely because it happened to be in the ship, why might not my lot prove the same? Oh, my heart! To think of becoming one of the crew, partaking their horrid destiny, and in due course dying to live again accurst and miraculously, my soul —as theirs—existing in my body like one of those feeble lamps with which the ancients illumined their tombs!

But I was young and was not without an Englishman's courage. I could gaze backwards and perceive in my life no sin such as should fill me with remorse and hopelessness

in a time like this. I believed in my
Creator's goodness, and reaching my darksome cabin, I knelt down and prayed, and
after awhile recollected myself and felt the
warmth of my former spirit.

I was mighty pleased to recover my own
clothes; they gave me back the sense of my
being my true self again, whereas the mas-
querading attire Vanderdecken had lent me
occasioned a wretched feeling as of belonging
to the ship. When I had shifted myself, I
neatly folded the captain's coat, breeches and
the rest, and then sat down on my bed
to think over my conversation with Miss
Dudley. What to credit, what to make of
her, I hardly knew. She was so beautiful
where all was ugly, so fresh where all was
decayed, so young where all was withered, so
radiant where all was darksome that, on
board such a ship as this, that had been con-
signed to the most dreadful doom the imagination of man could conceive of, how was I

to know that she was not some part of the
scheme of retribution—a sweet and dazzling
tantaliser, a mocker of the home affections of
the miserable ship's company, a lovely em-
bodiment of the spirit of life to serve some
purpose of an inscrutable nature in its influence upon such spiritual vitality as was
permitted to the corpse-like beings who
navigated this Death Ship.

But this was a fleeting fancy only, and
was rendered utterly ridiculous by recurrence
to her transporting figure, the golden warmth
of her hair and complexion, and above all to
the fragility of her lineaments, which stamped
her mortal. No! her story was the truth
itself; but this I understood, if Vanderdecken
were never to comprehend his doom, there
was stern assurance of his holding the girl to
his ship until she died ; because, as she had
pointed out, he had adopted her and desired
to take her home, and would never understand he was powerless to do so, even should

time represent the truth to him in her face, should she ever grow old enough for wrinkles and grey hairs.

Had I been sent to deliver her? God knoweth, I thought. Yet, what was my own case? Would they refuse to let me leave them? Well, that idea did not frighten me, for he is a poor sailor who cannot find a means of escape from a ship he dislikes, even though she should be commanded by Old Nick himself. But suppose they compelled me to go, set me ashore in their boat, or hailed some unsuspecting vessel that would receive me. I should then be powerless to rescue Imogene from this frightful situation, for as to subsequently helping to succour her, first of all I doubted whether I should find a sailor in any part of the world willing to ship for a cruise in search of Vanderdecken's craft, and next, even if I should be able to range a line-of-battle ship alongside this venerable frame, how should human artillery advantage us in such a conflict? 'Twould be but another defiance of the Divine intention, and what mariner was to be found who would embark on any adventure against this dread Spectre of the Deep when, by so doing, he would feel that he was fighting a Vengeance which would swiftly deal with him for so great an act of impiety?

However, no good could come of meditations of this kind in that gloomy cabin filled with the echoes of the groaning in the hold and the washing and shocks of the seas without. I felt a seaman's curiosity to have a good look at a ship of which there were a thousand stories afloat in every forecastle throughout the world, and so I climbed through the hatch on deck, dressed in the style in which I had made my first appearance. The second mate, Antony Arents, conned the vessel, standing near the helm with his arms folded in a sullen, moody posture, even so as to resemble a man turned into stone. Vanderdecken was at the weather-rail, erect and noble-looking, his legs parted in the attitude of a stride that he might balance himself to the rolling deck. He stared fixedly to the windward, his great beard, disparted, blowing like smoke over either shoulder, and his brows lowered into a contemptuous scowl upon his sharp, burning eyes. The ship was under the same canvas I had before noticed on her. Her yards were as closely pointed to the wind as the lee braces could bring them, but whereas in our time a square-rigged vessel close-hauled can be brought to within six points, that is to say, if the gale be north she can be made to head east-north-east, yet this ship, as I easily gathered without looking at the compass, lay no closer than eight-and-a-half or nine points, the wind blowing west-north-west and we lying by as close as the trim of the yards would suffer us, at about south-by-west.

In short, we were being driven at the rate

of some three or four miles an hour dead to
leeward, broadside on. Now, as I am writing
this in the main that all mariners may have a
just and clear conception of the sort of ship
Vanderdecken's vessel is, I particularly desire
that this matter of her not being able to sail
within eight or nine points of the wind be
carefully noted; for, then you shall understand how fully with her own tackling, and
yards and canvas, she helps out and fulfils
her doom.

If ever you have read the account of
my Lord Anson's voyage round the world,
you will recollect, in the second chapter of
Book II., the narrative, given at length, of
the time occupied by the Gloucester in fetching and casting anchor off Juan Fernandez.
She could make no way at all in beating or
reaching. She was first sighted from the
island on the 21st of June; she was still striving against the head wind on the 9th of July;
then she was blown away, and reappeared on

the 16th, and it was not until the 23rd of
that month that she was seen opening the
north-west point of the bay with a flowing
sail, which means that she had a fair wind,
and which may also be said to signify that
had the wind not favoured her she might
have gone on struggling for years without
making the island. Think, now, of a vessel
very nearly fitted as our ships are rigged,
occupying thirty-two days—a whole month
and a day atop—in covering a distance
which, when the Gloucester was first sighted,
was reckoned at four leagues!

Is it, then, surprising that a vessel constructed considerably more than a century
earlier than the ships of Anson's squadron, in
an age when the art of building was little
understood, when a ship's hull was as tall as
a great castle, when all things aloft were
ponderous, when the immense beam, helped
yet by the wide channels, gave such a spread
to the shrouds that they could make of the

breeze no more than a beam wind when braced up as sharp as the yards would come —is it surprising, I say, that this Dutchman, so constructed, should never be able to contend with a contrary wind? I am the more pleased to point this out because I have heard it particularly affirmed that if Vanderdecken were a good seaman he would laugh at a north-wester though there should be no other wind in those seas; for he need do nothing but make a long board to the south, to as far, say, as fifty degrees, in order, with his starboard tacks aboard, to pass the Cape and enter the Atlantic, where he would probably catch the south-east trade wind and so make good his return. But this presupposes no Sentence, even if the ship were capable of sailing close-hauled.

To resume. Neither the captain, nor the second mate, nor the seaman at the tiller, taking the least notice of me, I determined to keep myself to myself till it should please

Vanderdecken to address me; so I got under
the lee of the house where I had conversed
with the captain before breakfast, and gazed
about.   It was as dirty a day as ever I
remember — the heavens of the colour of
drenched granite, the sea-line swallowed up
in spray and haze, out of which there came
rolling to the ship endless processions of
olive - coloured, prodigious combers.   The
storming aloft was a perpetual thunder.
Upon every rope the gale split with a shriek,
and there was a dreary clattering of the cordage, and as the vessel swang her spars to
windward, an edge of peculiar and hurricane-
like fierceness would be put into the wind,
as though it were driven outrageously mad
by the stubborn swing of the masts against
its howling face.   Nothing was in sight save
over against our weather-quarter a Cape hen,
poised on such easy wings that the appearance of the bird made a wonder of the weight
of the blast; its solitariness gave a heavy

desolation to the aspect of the pouring, warring scene of frothing summits and roaring
hollows. The reefed courses under which
the vessel lay were dark with wet from the
showering of the sea, of which great, green,
glittering masses striking the weather-bow,
raised such a smoke of crystals all about the
forecastle that the vessel looked to be on
fire with the steam-like, voluminous whiteness soaring there.

There were a few men on the decks that
way, muffled up to their noses ; but I did not
see them speak to one another nor go about
any kind of work. They had the same self-
engrossed, nay, entranced air that was visible
in those, such as the two mates and Vanderdecken, whom I had already observed. The
ship offered an amazing picture as she soared
and sank upon the billows, half-hidden by
storms of froth swept by the wind betwixt
the masts with wilder screamings than a
hundred mad-houses could make. The great

barricaded tops, her spritsail topmast standing up out of another top at the end of the bowsprit—she had no jibboom—and the long yard, after the lateen-style, on her mizzenmast, gave her so true a look of the age in which she had been built that it would be impossible for any sailor to see her and not know what ship she was. None other resembling her has been afloat since the age of William III., nor is it conceivable that the like of her will ever be seen again.

CHAPTER XIX.

I HAD been on deck about a quarter of an hour when Vanderdecken, who all this time was standing motionless at the rail looking —as who shall tell with what fancies in him and what visions—at the windward sea, came down to the lee of the house as though he all along knew I was there, though I can swear he never once turned nor appeared to see me, and said—

" Is the lady in the cabin ?"

" She went to her room, sir," I replied.

" Did she tell you her story ?" he said, bringing his beard to its place with both hands, and viewing me with a severity that I began to think might be as much

owing to the cast of his features as to his
nature.

I replied that she had told me how he had
met with her in an open boat, how her
parents had perished, and how he had felt a
father's pity and love for her and was taking
her home.

"To adopt her," he exclaimed. "She
shall be a child of mine. My wife will soon
love her, and she will be a sister to my
daughters. She has no relatives, and such
beauty and sweetness of heart as hers must
be cared for, since how does the world commonly serve such graces when they meet in a
friendless woman?"

Surely, thought I, he that can talk thus
cannot be endevilled! And yet does not
the great Milton bestow the tenderness of
a sister and a daughter on Sin when she
reconciles Satan and Death? Something of
human nature there must ever be even in
those who most strictly merit Heaven's chas-

tisement; and the lustre of the glory in our beginning, though it wane till its glow is no brighter than the dim, fiery crawlings upon this ship's side at night, is never utterly extinguished in the blackest spirit of us all.

I had no desire to talk of Miss Dudley lest I should put him into a passion by some remark touching the number of years she had now been on board, or by blundering in some other-like manner. If she was to escape through me it behoved me to keep my thoughts mighty close and secret, for let what would be the state of being he had entered into in two centuries of existence, his eyes were like a burning-glass, as though he could focus by them the fires of suspicion and scorch a hole through your body to your soul to learn what was passing there. So putting on an easy manner and throwing a glance aloft and around, I said, "I fear, mynheer, you find weather of this kind strain your ship a good deal."

" Like all vessels she will work in such seas as this," he replied.

" How often is she careened ?" I asked.

" How often should she need it, think you ?" he replied, with sudden temper.

I said, warily, " I cannot imagine."

" I have commanded the Braave for five voyages," said he, softening a little, "and only once—that is during the second voyage —did she prove leaky. But this voyage she has been troublesome, and I have had to careen her twice."

Twice only, thought I ; but you could see that his memory had been shaped so as to fit his doom, and that remembrance of all that befell him and his crew from the time when his sentence was first pronounced faded almost as swiftly as they happened, like clouds upon the blankness of the heavens, so that the very changes that would illustrate the passage of time to you or me, such as the alteration in the rigs and shapes of the ships he met, or the growth into womanhood of the girl he had rescued, would be as unmeaning to him and his fellows as to men without memory. Yet was it manifestly part of the Curse that he should have a keen and bright recollection of his house, his family, Amsterdam, the politics and wars of his age and the like. For if the faculty was wholly dead in him, he would be but as a corpse without that craving for home which perpetuates his doom.

"Is there any good spot for careening on the coast, east of the Cape?" said I, eager to gather all I could touching the practices and inner life of this wondrous ship without appearing inquisitive.

He answered, "Yes, there is one good place, 'tis in a bay; I cannot name it, but it is to be found by the peculiar shape of the mountains at its back. If ever you should be in these seas and need to careen, choose that place, for besides that you may refresh your crew with, and lay in a good store of—when

in season—oranges, plums, wild apricot,
lemons, plantains, and other fruits, with abun-
dance of such fish as cod, hake, and mullet,
and comforts and dainties such as plovers,
partridges, guinea-fowl, and bustards; you will
there find a salt spring, the water of which,
on boiling, yields salt enough for any quantity of curing, and what should not be less
useful to you as a mariner to know is, that
about the shore you find scattered a kind of
munjack which, when boiled with sand and
tempered with oil, is as good as pitch for
paying your seams with."

So, thought I, and thither, then, is it that
you are led when your ship needs to be overhauled or when your provisions run low.
With oakum worked from such ropes as he
would find on abandoned ships, and the munjack he spoke about, he would have no
trouble in keeping the frame of the vessel
tight, more especially as the supernatural
quality that was in his own life was in that of

his ship likewise, so that the timber stood as did his skin, albeit the one would often need repairs just as the body of the other was sustained by meat and drink.

"I thank you for your information, captain," said I.

"If," he continued, "you let the plantain dry it will crush into an excellent flour. The cakes we had at breakfast were formed of plantain-flour."

"It is wonderful," said I, "how the mariner forces the sea and the land that skirts it to supply his needs."

"Ay," he exclaimed. "It is as you say. But no sailors surpass the Dutch in this particular direction."

It seemed as if he would go on speaking, but, looking, that I might attend to his words, I observed that the whole man, with amazing suddenness, appeared to undergo a change. He stood motionless, gazing at the leeward sea, his features fixed, not the

faintest working in them, and nothing stirring but his beard.　He was like one in a
fit, save for the frightful vitality he got from
the glare in his eyes, which were rooted as
though they beheld a phantom.　I drew away
from him with a shudder, for his aspect now
was the most terrible revelation of his monstrous and unearthly existence that had been
made to me.　The change was of the violence
of a catalepsy, and this quick transition from
the intelligent, if death-like, looks of a man,
speaking of homely matters to a mute, petri-
fied figure, to which the fire of the eyes im-
parted an inexpressible element of horror, so
terrified me that I felt the sweat-drops in
the palms of my hands.　As to reasoning
on this condition of his, why, I could make
nothing of it.　It looked as if the death that
was in his flesh and bones, finding his spirit,
or whatever it was that informed him, languid, as the senses became through grief or
sickness, asserted its powers till it was driven

into its hiding-place again by the re-quicken-
ing of the supernatural element that possessed
him. It was also apparent that this unnatural
gift of life did but give vitality to a corpse;
and that even as a disinterred body that
still wears the very tint of life, as though but
just dead, falls into dust on the air of
Heaven touching it, so do I strictly believe
that Vanderdecken and his crew would instantly crumble into ashes, which the wind
would disperse, were the power that keeps
them intelligent and capable of moving
suspended. By which I mean that they
would not decay slowly, · as the dead in
Nature do, but that they would dissolve into
dust as men who deceased a hundred years
ago.

These thoughts are not gay. But what
think you of the reality? Never could I
so fully compass all the horror of the Curse
as now, when I turned my gaze from the
figure at my side, majestic in his marble

motionlessness and alive in the eyes only, to
the strained, grey, streaming ancient ship,
tossing her forking bowsprit to the sullen
gloom on high, bringing her aged, patched
and dingy courses, groaning at their tacks,
with a sulky thunder against the screaming
gale, as though their hollows dimly reverber-
ated yet the cannonading of the vanished
fleets of Blake and Tromp ; washed by seas
which fled in snow-storms over her forward
decks, heavily and dismally rolling broadside
to the wind that was blowing her with
diabolic stubbornness back along the liquid
path that she had so lately sailed over!
Think of such a life as this, never-ending!
Great Mercy!   Would not even a year of such
a struggle prove to us distracting.   Oh, 'tis a
merciful provision indeed that these poor
wretches should have had all sense of time
killed in them, and that their punishment
should lie in a perpetual cheating of hope too
short-lived as a remembrance to break their

hearts. Yet there were now two persons in this Death Ship to whom such solace as was permitted to the accurst crew would not be granted, and who, if they could not get away from the vessel, would have to lead a more terrible life than even that of the Dutch mariners, unless they destroyed themselves as Captain Skevington had. And for some time I could think of nothing but how I was to rescue Miss Dudley and make my own escape, for one thing I had already resolved: never to leave the girl alone in this ship.

CHAPTER XX.

THERE was nothing in sight. Indeed, in that thick gale a vessel would have had to come within a mile of us to be visible. As Vanderdecken neither stirred nor spoke to me, I feared he might take it ill if I hung by his side, for how was I to tell but that he might consider I should regard the withdrawal of his attention as a hint to begone I therefore walked aft, the second mate no more heeding me than if I had been as viewless as the air, whilst the helmsman, after turning a small pair of glassy eyes upon me, stained with veins, directed them again at the sea over the bow, his face as sullenly thoughtful as the others, albeit he handled the tiller with good judgment, "meeting her," as we sailors say, when she needed it, and holding a very clean and careful luff.

My curiosity being great I ventured to peep into the binnacle, or "bittacle" as it was formerly called, a fixed box or case for holding the mariner's compass. The card was very old-fashioned, as may be supposed, yet it swung to the movement of the ship, and I could not suppose that it was very inaccurate since by the aid of it they periodically made the land where they hunted for meat and filled their casks. As neither Vanderdecken nor Antony Arents offered to hinder me from roaming about, I determined, since I was about it, to take a good look at this Death Ship. I examined the swivels which were very green with decay, and tried to revolve one on its pivot, but found that it was not to be stirred. The tiller had been a very noble piece of timber, but now presented the aspect of rottenness that all the rest of the wood in the ship had, yet it had been very elegantly carved, and numerous flourishes still overran it, though the meaning of the devices was not to be come at. The rudder head worked in a great helm-port, through which a corpulent man of eighteen stone might have slipped fair into the sea underneath. The gale made a melancholy screeching in the skeleton lantern, and I wondered they did not unship the worthless thing and heave it overboard. I looked over the side and as far down as I could carry my sight, and I observed that the ship was of a sickly sallow colour, not yellow—indeed, of no hue that I could give a name to, though the original tint a painter might conjecture by guessing what colour would yield this nameless pallidness after years and years of washing seas and the burning of the sun.

I then thought I would step forward, not much minding the washing of the seas there, and passed Vanderdecken very cautiously, ready to stop if he should look at me, but he remained in a trance, like a stone figure, all the life of him gone into his eyes, which glared burning and terrible at the same part of the ocean at which he stared when I first observed him stirless; so I stepped past and descended to the quarter-deck, where there was nothing to see, and thence to the upper deck.

Here, near the mainmast, were two pumps of the pattern I recollected noticing in a ship that had been built in 1722, and that was afloat and hearty and earning good money in 1791. In front of the mast lay two boats, one within the other, the under one on chocks, both of the same pattern, namely, square stern and stem, with lengths of the gunwales projecting like horns. The top one, for I could not see the inside of the lower boat, had been painted originally a bright scarlet; she contained seats and half-a-dozen of oars short and long, all with immensely broad blades, which had also been painted a bright red. The rusty guns, the ends of gear snaking in the froth along the scuppers, the cumbersomeness of the blocks of the maintack, along with the other furniture of that groaning and half-bursting sail, the grey old cask answering for a scuttlebutt lashed to the larboard side, the ancientness of the tarpauling over the great hatch ; these, and a score of other details it would tease you to hear me name, gave a most dismal and wretched appearance to all this part of the tossed, drenched, spray-clouded fabric labouring under a sky that had darkened since the morning, and against whose complexion the edges of the sails showed with a raw and sickly pallor, whilst above swung the great barricaded tops and the masts and yards to and fro, to and fro, how drearily and wearily !

The bulwarks being very high, enabled me to dodge the seas as I crept forwards, and presently I came abreast of the foremast,

where stood Jans, the boatswain, along with
three or four seamen, taking the shelter of a
sort of hutch, built very strong, whence pro-
ceeded sounds of the grunting of hogs, and
the muttering of geese, hens and the like.
As I needed an excuse to be here—for these
fellows believed the time to be that of Cromwell and Blake, and looked upon an Englishman as an enemy, and, therefore, might round
upon me angrily for offering to overhaul their
ship—I said to Jans, in my civillest manner—

"Are the men who rescued me last night
here? I shall be glad to thank them."

"Yonder's Houtmann," said he, bluntly;
"the other's below."

I turned to the man named Houtmann,
and saw in him an old sailor of perhaps
three-score, with a drooped head, his hands
in his pockets, a worn, wrinkled, melancholy
face, his complexion, like that of the others,
of the grave; he was dressed in boots, loose
yellow, tarpaulin trousers, and a frock of the

same material ; he had a pilot-coat on, a good sou'-west cap—such as I myself wore aboard the Saracen—and there was a stout shawl around his neck.

I put out my hand, and said, " Houtmann, let an English sailor thank a brave Hollander of his own calling for his life."

He did not smile—showed himself, by not so much as a twitch in his face sensible of my speech, save that in the most lifeless manner in the world he held out his hand, which I took ; but I was glad to let it fall. If ever a hand had the chill of death to freeze mortal flesh, his had that coldness. No other man's skin in that ship had I before touched, though my arm had been seized by Vanderdecken, and this contact makes one of the most biting memories of that time. Will you suppose that the coldness was produced by the wet and the wind ? Alas! he withdrew his hand from his pocket ; but, even had he raised it from a block of ice, you would not, in the bitter bleakness of the flesh, have felt, as I did, the death in his veins, had he been as I was.

The others were variously attired, in such clothes as you would conceive a ship's slop-chest would be fitted with from pickings of vessels encountered and ransacked in a hundred and fifty years. They had all of them a Dutch cast of countenance, one looking not more than thirty, another forty, and so on. But there was something in them— though God knows if my life were the stake I should not be able to define it—that, backed by the movements, complexions and the like, made you see that with them time had become eternity, and that their exteriors were no more significant of the years they could count than the effigy on the tomb of a man represents the dust of him.

"It blows hard," said I to Jans, making the most of my stock of Dutch, and resolved to confront each amazing experience as it befel me with a bold face. "But the Braave is a stout ship and makes excellent weather."

"So think the rats," exclaimed Houtmann, addressing Jans.

"A plague on the rats!" cried Jans. "There's but one remedy : when we get to Table Bay the hold must be smoked with sulphur."

"I never knew rats multiply as they do in this ship," said one of the sailors, named Kryns ; "had we been ten years making the passage from Batavia, the vermin could not have increased more rapidly."

"Where do the crew sleep?" said I.

Jans pointed over his shoulder with his thumb to a hatch abreast of the after-end of the forecastle bulwark. The cover was over it, for there the spray was constantly shooting up like steam from boiling water, and filling the iron-hard hollow of the foresail with wet which showered from under the arched foot-rope in whole thunderstorms of rain. Other-

wise I should have asked leave to go below
and explore the forecastle, for no part of this
ship could, I thought, be more curious than
the place in which her crew lived, and I
particularly desired to see how they slept,
nay, to see them sleeping and to observe the
character of their beds, whether hammocks
or bunks, and their chests or bags for their
clothes.

I said, " It will be dark enough down there
with the hatch closed ?"

" Ay," said the youngest-looking of the
seamen, named Abraham Bothma—I took
down their names afterwards from Imogene's
dictation, conceiving that the mentioning of
them would prove of interest to any de-
scendants of theirs in Holland into whose
hands this narrative might chance to fall—
" but we keep a lamp always burning."

" But should you run short of oil !" said I,
timorously, for I had made up my mind to
pretend to one and all that I believed they

had sailed from Batavia in the preceding year, and the question was a departure from that resolution.

"Oil is easily got," exclaimed Jans, roughly. "What use do you English make of the porpoise and the grampus? Is not the sea-bird full of it? And fish you in any bay along the coast 'twixt Natal and Cape Town, and I'll warrant you livers enough to keep your lamps burning for a voyage round the world. And what ship with coppers aboard can be wanting in slush?"

"Heer Jans," said I, "I am a sailor and love to hear the opinions of persons of my own calling. Therefore I would ask you, do not you consider your ship greatly hampered forward by yonder sprit-topmast and the heavy yards there?" And to render myself perfectly intelligible, I pointed to the mast that I have already described as being fixed upright at the end of the bowsprit, rising, so to speak, out of a round top there, and

having a smaller top on the upper end of
it.

"How would you have her rigged?" asked
he, in a sneering manner.

"Why," said I, cautiously, "as most of
the ships you meet are rigged—with a jibboom upon which you can set more useful
canvas than spritsails."

On this, Bothma said, "Let your country
rig its ships as it chooses, they will find the
Dutch know more about the sea and the art
of navigating and commanding it than your
nation has stomach for."

I could have smiled at this, but the voice
of the man, the deadness of his face, the
terrifying life in his eyes, the sombre gravity
of the others, standing about me like people
in their sleep, were such a corrective of
humour as might have made a braver man
than I am tremble. I dared not go on talking with them, indeed, their looks caused me
to fear for my senses, so without further ado

I walked aft and entered the cabin hoping to find warmth and recovery for my mind in the beauty and conversation of Imogene.

The cabin was deserted. The darkness of the sky made it very gloomy, and what with its meagre furniture, the unhealthy colouring of its walls, trappings of gilt and handwork, once I daresay very brilliant and delightful, but now as rueful as a harlequin's faded dress seen by the sun, it was a most depressing interior, particularly in such weather as was then storming, when the ceaseless thunder of bursting surges drove shock after shock of tempestuous sound through the resonant fabric, and when the shrieking of the wind, not only in the rigging but along the floor of the stormy sky itself, was like the frantic tally-hoing of demons to the million hounds of the blast.

Not knowing how to pass the time, I went to the old, framed pictures upon the sides, and found them to be panels fitted to the ship's plank, and framed so as to form as much a part of the structure as the carving on her stern would be. But time, neglect, dirt or damp—one or all—had so befouled or darkened the surfaces that most of them were more like the heads of tar barrels than paintings. Yet here and there I managed to witness a glimmering survival of the artist's work ; one representing the fish market at Amsterdam, such of the figures as were plain exhibiting plenty of humour ; another a Dutch East Indiaman, of Vanderdecken's period, sailing along with canvas full, streamers blowing, and the Batavian colours standing out large from the ensign staff ; a third was a portrait, but nothing was left of it save a nose whose ruddy tip time had evidently fallen in love with, for there it still glowed, a mouth widely distended with laughter, and one merry little eye, the other having sunk like a star in the dark cloud that overspread most of this panel. This, I supposed, had

been the portrait of a sailor, for so much of
the remainder as was determinable all related
to Amsterdam and things nautical. Having
made this dismal round, I sat me down at the
table, sternly and closely watched by the
parrot, whose distressing, croaking assurance
I had no wish to hear, she being my only
company if I except the clock, whose hoarse
ticking was audible above the gale, and the
skeleton skulking inside, whose hourly resur-
rection I was now in the temper to as greatly
dislike as the bird's iterative denunciation.

I wondered how the young lady contrived
to pass her time. Had she books? If so,
they would doubtless be dull performances in
old Dutch, fat and wormy volumes bound
in hard leather—as sluggish in their matter
as a canal, and very little calculated to amuse
a spirited girl. Evidently, in the five years
she had been sailing with Vanderdecken, she
had learnt what she knew of Dutch; she
spoke fluently, and with a good accent,

though, to be sure, it was the Dutch of 1650.
I constantly directed my eyes towards her
cabin, in the hope of seeing her emerge, for
I felt mighty dull and sad, and longed for
the sight of her fair and golden beauty ; and
all the while I was wondering how she had
endured, without losing her mind, the dreadful imprisonment she had undergone and
was yet undergoing, and the still more
fearful association of the captain and his
men.

I also employed myself in turning over
several schemes for escaping with her, but
nothing that was really practicable offered.
Suppose we met with an unsuspecting ship—
I mean a vessel that did not know we were
the craft that has been called the Flying
Dutchman—Vanderdecken, being willing to
get rid of me, sends me to her in a boat. I
cry out that there is a young lady left behind
breaking her heart for home, whereupon explanations would follow to prove the vessel

the Death Ship! What would happen? In all probability, if I had managed to board the vessel we met, her crew, to preserve her from the Curse, would fling me overboard. In any case, away they would run directly the truth was known. Indeed, acquainted as I was with the terror with which Vanderdecken was viewed by all classes of mariners, 'twas positive that, though he had no suspicion himself of the dread he inspired, the story that would have to be told concerning Miss Dudley to account for her detention in the Phantom Ship would end in resolving those we encountered to have nothing to do with either her or me, but to bear a hand and "up sticks!"

As to getting away with her in one of the Dutchman's boats, first, how was I to hoist the boat over the side unperceived? Next, suppose that was to be managed, then on his missing us would not Vanderdecken, a man of fierce resolution, hunt after and perhaps

find us, when I should be at the mercy of one
in whom there was a great deal of the devil,
and who, Heaven knows, could not revenge
himself more awfully than by keeping me in
his ship.   Several projects I thought of, and
then a strange idea came into my head.
Here was a girl without mother or father,
and, as I gathered, entirely friendless and
penniless, as indeed in this latter article she
could hardly help being as the child of a
sailor.   Suppose I should succeed in escaping
with her?   How could an association such as
ours end but in a wedding?   And did that
consideration agitate me?   Faith, though I
had only known her since this morning, I
reckoned, being young and in an especial
degree an admirer and lover of the kind of
beauty and sweetness this girl had in perfection, it would not need many days to pass
before my heart would be hers.

Forthwith my imagination grew sunny.
Many bright and delightful ideas occurred to

me. Would not my tremendous experience
find a glorious crowning in the hand of this
girl and her endowment by Vanderdecken,
who loved her, out of those chests of treasure
and coin which he had in his hold? Would
it be impossible for me to persuade him, say
after the next gale which blew him back from
Agulhas, to put us aboard some vessel homeward bound along with a chest of treasure for
his wife as an earnest of what was coming,
and so enable me to convey Miss Dudley
straight to Amsterdam there to await his
arrival? It was but a young man's fancy,
pretentious and inconsistent with my opinion
of the captain's temper and his ignorance of
the Curse that lay on him; and it was not
perhaps strictly honest. Though if you come
to consider that his doom would never suffer
him to use the riches he had in his ship, nor
to know whether I had faithfully carried Miss
Dudley to his house on the Buitenkant—
where I afterwards heard he was living when

he sailed—you will not judge me harshly for thus idly and merrily dreaming.

I was in the midst of this castle-building when the hour of noon was struck by the clock. I watched the figure of Death hewing with his lance, but with an abstracted eye, my mind being full of gay and hopeful fancies. But the moment the last stroke had rung, the parrot cried out :—

"Wy Zyn al Verdomd !"

with so fierce an energy that it broke up my thoughts as you destroy a spider's web by passing your finger through it, and I dropped my chin on to my breast with my spirits dashed.

END OF VOLUME I.

www.ingramcontent.com/pod-product-compliance
Lightning Source LLC
Chambersburg PA
CBHW021039030726
47496CB00006B/1605